T0279959

VILLA E

ALSO BY JANE ALISON

Meander, Spiral, Explode: Design and Pattern in Narrative

Nine Island

Change Me: Stories of Sexual Transformation from Ovid

The Sisters Antipodes: A Memoir

Natives and Exotics: A Novel

The Marriage of the Sea: A Novel

The Love-Artist: A Novel

VILLA

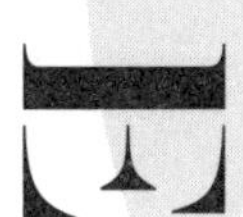

A NOVEL

Jane Alison

Liveright Publishing Corporation

A Division of W. W. Norton & Company
Independent Publishers Since 1923

This is a work of historical fiction. Apart from the well-known actual people, events, and locales that figure in the narrative, all names, characters, places, and incidents are the products of the author's imagination or are used fictitiously. Any resemblance to current events or locales, or to living persons, is entirely coincidental.

Copyright © 2024 by Jane Alison

All rights reserved
Printed in the United States of America
First Edition

For information about permission to reproduce selections from this book, write to Permissions, Liveright Publishing Corporation, a division of W. W. Norton & Company, Inc., 500 Fifth Avenue, New York, NY 10110

For information about special discounts for bulk purchases, please contact W. W. Norton Special Sales at specialsales@wwnorton.com or 800-233-4830

Manufacturing by Lake Book Manufacturing
Book design by Daniel Lagin
Production manager: Louise Mattarelliano

ISBN 978-1-324-09505-7

Liveright Publishing Corporation
500 Fifth Avenue, New York, N.Y. 10110
www.wwnorton.com

W. W. Norton & Company Ltd.
15 Carlisle Street, London W1D 3BS

1 2 3 4 5 6 7 8 9 0

VILLA E

FRIDAY, 27 AUGUST 1965

Here, where continents once split apart and a fresh sea poured between, where another continent then barged north, crashed into the new seabed and old land beside it, and forced them up, smashing and shocking them miles into the sky until they'd become a huge jagged mountain range shouldering over Europe; here, on the Ligurian coast, the Blue Coast, the south coast of France, where the Alps cataract into the Mediterranean, on a slab of stone still holding the memory of tiny creatures that lived and died and drifted downward, a memory seen in whorls, fans, and rings; here on this stone slab jutting from earthen terraces into the sea sits a slim white house, moored like a yacht, modern in the ancient sun.

Low and bright, the house has a band of window along its wide deck, a life preserver slung to the rail; on the roof is a mast with tattered banner. The villa's elegant and worn and somehow looks shy. It's made of fine concrete, liquid stone: the woman who built the house poured it. And she gave it a name in code, her initials around those of the man she loved, the one for whom she made the place. But he's long gone, and she, Eileen, left the house even before he did. She's come back only once—no, twice. But just this week she swam in the pebbled cove below and looked up for a hard moment.

In this wide arcing cove, waves roll in, crash on the pebbles, wash back to sea, roll in. The pebbles are gray or white or black, striped or zigged or pure. They've been jostled so long they're smooth as eggs.

Above the pebbles, above slabs of stone, on the earthen terraces beyond the house, crouch several wooden buildings, ringing it as if set there to watch. Right behind the villa is a brightly painted shed with holiday rooms; beside this shed, the fish place; adjoining it, his little cabanon; and ten paces away, the plank shack where he works. It's barely dawn, no one to be seen, but on a table inside this shack are traces: papers, eraser shreds, a shell, two bones. Sketches of women are tacked to a wall: naked women on their knees or backs, breasts thrust up, big rumps. But back to the cabanon, for it's the heart of this precinct: it's small, dark, made of rough logs, with mirrored shutters reflecting the view and a palm frond nailed to the door. Inside this dim wooden cube he made himself, Le Grand is asleep and snoring.

NOW THE SUN'S UP, FINE HOT RAYS SLANTING THROUGH EUCALYPTS, lemons, and pines. Le Grand snores again, snorts awake. After a moment he sits, reaches for his glasses. Then stands, limps across the floor, gropes for the shutter, pulls it back.

And here's a square of brilliant blue.

His own Mediterranean.

Round glasses, boulder head, he stands naked with fist on hip and gazes out, smelling of rank old man. A cluster of scars winds about a thick thigh; between his legs, his soft little squid. He pets it gently.

Dear old bad friend, he thinks. Let's take you swimming.

Forget Hindermeyer. Le Grand has woken lighter than he's been in weeks, as though something's been set loose inside, and he's lusty to be in salt water, enveloped in surging cool sea. To plunge!

He pulls a black scrap of swimsuit from the peg and steps in, wobbling as he aims foot into hole. Stands, straightens, tucks the cloth about his waist.

Loincloth, he thinks. Sacred garb.

No, not sacred: sanctified. Or almost, once he's done.

He steps outside, and it really is a stepping out. Glossy pine needles beneath bare feet, fresh smell of tamarisk, buzz of cicadas, glaze of sea.

Architect-sculptor-swimmer-diver: Mediterranean man.

This earthen terrace, with his cabin and workshop ten paces away, falls to another terrace, then another and another, once carefully planted but now a jungle of olive trees, pines, cactuses, and yuccas, until terraces give way to jagged stone that drops into sloshing surf. Above, blazing blue. Far behind, stone-flesh cliff: here's where the Alps crash into the sea.

Le Grand strides up his curving concrete steps to the path that runs between his enclave and the train tracks, the path that takes one up to the station or down steep steps to the cove. His enclave: pleasing always to regard it from above as he paces past: his workshop, then his cabin, the fish place adjoining as if his own kitchen, then the jolly shed of holiday rooms, and that white villa just beyond. Ridged concrete beneath his feet. Concrete—*béton brut*—he still loves it. Of course it's crude; that's its allure; only a fool would not understand. And anyway there is a fine beauty, too, if you must have fineness: look how concrete that's been poured and formed between planks of wood holds the whorl and grain of the living tree. Like a fossil we can make.

Onward through pines and buzzing cicadas to the steps leading down to the pebbled cove. The pebbles still hold the coolness of dawn, although he barely feels them underfoot, when yesterday they bruised his arches. He's truly grown more light.

He drops towel and glasses, limps to where water frills smooth sand, nearly melts at its spring and give.

He is a child at the beach. The desire to sculpt and mold, to dig and make: enormous! The impulse that has driven him always. An itching in palms to print himself upon matter, to form, to mark, to plunge.

But wait, not yet. Give Doctor H a thought. Get used to the water's chill first, even on this late August morning.

He turns, water jostling at knees, and gazes over the slab of rock, up to his cabin, the rest. Then to the villa, its mast, its glass spiral.

From here, you can't see all he's done to it.

Slim as a yacht, somehow shy.

A correction from you seems necessary

Well, all right.

He turns to the sea, bends at cracking knees. Architect-sculptor-swimmer-diver! A sea-lion splash, and he's enveloped. Head under, eyes open raw to the greenish haze and sting, then up, salt wet running from his mouth as he lashes his head left and right, casting forward, clutching liquid, legs kicking, diaperlike swimsuit lifting away as his hips rock side to side and water furls through the folds.

He can feel it still, the first time he swam in the sea—forty years ago?—water parting to his hands. Flesh first parted for him then, too. His Von was almost the first and almost the last, but so many Scyllas between.

Well, all done now.

Head to left, head to right, water sloshing into mouth as the cliff, shaggy greenery, villa blur in and out of view.

Soon done with all that too, clean again.

Heavy sound of breaths in his underwater ear, knees feeling stiff, stone.

Strange that in the water he's begun to feel heavy, when up in the air, so light. Face under, face out, legs kick, arms slash. Blurred sunlit cliff, ragged breaths, plumes of cold.

Then, inside: a pain like blanching.

And he thinks, *Of course.*

1

SATURDAY, 21 AUGUST 1965

Around the scalloped limestone coast, west of Menton, west of Cap M, west of the cabanon and villa, past Monaco and Nice, and farther west to the gulf of St. T, then inland, Eileen's in her study-lounge gathering notebooks and paper while Pruny waits outside. Low fieldstone walls, sliding glass doors, torrents of sun, agave looking like petrified sea grass, two olive trees, baked earth. Eileen's third house, the last.

Sure you don't mind going back there? Pruny calls.

Eileen looks out, her niece looks in, and if you blur, it's mirrors gazing at each other, but for forty years. Pruny tall and pale with far-apart pale eyes, small serious mouth, standing in paint-spattered trousers; Eileen a weathered version, same eyes, same mouth, roll of paper in hand, one lens of her glasses blackened. Tousled black hair, tousled silver.

You really don't mind going back there, Pruny says as she steps inside. Going back alone?

Eileen selects markers, fat ones in different colors, drops them into her satchel. Back there. Meaning her hill house near Menton, the second house she built and second one she had to leave. The man who bought it ten years ago, Graham (famous painter, friend of Pruny's, did Churchill), was thinking he'd like an extension, which of course the house's designer should do. But only if she was up to it, he'd added, to which Eileen and Pruny snorted. But he'd agreed to clear away for the week so Eileen could go see what she thought. And alone, alone would be just right. So Pruny had traveled down to St. T from London to watch the tortoise and vines, and Louise would take her first holiday in nearly half a century, while Eileen went back to her old house, her second house, the one she called Time.

Eileen considers her pencils, chooses five with the softest lead, then a fan of them in different hues.

Why would I mind going back? she says.

Oh, Auntie.

The driving?

Yes, of course, with your eye, but mostly just being there again, you know.

Eileen picks up her typewriter, sets it on the table near the door. It was all long ago, she says.

Ah yes, says Pruny, who's learnt dryness well, her eyes emanating a kind of dry light. Those far-apart eyes so full of thought, that mouth so small and fixed, her stubbornness against living the regular life plain in her jaw: no need even to squint to see her as Eileen at that age. Data running through flesh, Eileen thinks, turning out the same models.

Well I'm glad you're going, Pruny says. I won't be patronizing and call it brave. But I'll check on you, so do pick up the phone. I can come whenever you like.

Yes, Eileen says, but no, dear. Just mind the tortoise. And vines.

Ah thank you, she says to Louise, who has come in with a look as dry as Pruny's in her tolerant eyes, and in her arms a basket.

Some things, Louise says, by which Eileen knows she means food, which Eileen of course hadn't thought about, and hopefully also means drink.

All right, says Eileen. All set.

She's reaching for the basket, satchel over her shoulder, and the typewriter and rolls of paper, but Louise holds on to the basket, shares a glance with Pruny, and the two of them gather up everything and help Eileen out the door to the car.

All right, says Eileen again, thank you, bye now—

But will you go see it? asks Pruny.

What?

The *sea* house.

Quick shake of head, and Eileen steps into her Morgan, this one called Totor 2.

Then what about *him*? asks Pruny.

Eileen bangs the door shut.

Well, you might run into him. This could be the time to—

But now the steering wheel's hot in Eileen's hands, the key's turned to a roar, and she feels nothing but go-go-go.

HALF AN HOUR LATER SHE'S MOTORING ALONG THE CORNICHE, THE sea a vast blue haze to the right, hot wind whipping around her. Of course she's not meant to drive because of her eye and the shake in her hands, but here she is blasting from St. T to Menton, racing half a mile above the coast and two below the last Alp.

The color of the sky! And the sea! Glorious.

Her first time back this way in ten years.

Silly question, does she mind.

Anyway, Eileen'd been lucky back then to sell the hill house, funds being low after remaking her furniture and reglazing the windows and resetting the tiles and so on, after the wreck the German soldiers and then looters had left. Her chairs smashed, drawings burnt, pajamas in a puddle of pee, trees hacked

Should not think this while driving the corniche.

The color of the sky! And the sea!

Of course the house's original designer should do it

But only if she's up to it

Ha.

Some ossify, others putrefy, all age. These words always in her head now, not hers, a writer's, Gide? But now they seem hers, spoken by her inner voice, just as the figures in your dreams are you, because who else could they be?

One of the things that's come full circle during her decades on earth: interest in the unconscious, dreams stepping full of color and monstrosity into art and films, and she likes that, the way old surrealism is now, what do they say, *psychedelia.*

Short dresses, bold bright patterns.

Mod.

She herself had been Modernism personified.

Rode a motorcycle, wore trousers, boots.

Walked around at times with a panther.

So fine to be spinning along the corniche this morning! Wind in her hair, sun on her cheek! Go-go-go as if she were thirty or even fifty again, scalloped coastline far below, all that gleaming sea! About to pass Cannes now—halfway there.

When she first came from Ireland decades ago, no Brit would

be caught here in the summertime heat. And now it's all yachts and stars and Brigitte Bardot and villas climbing the hills.

Let's stay focused on now. Watch the road, these curves—but look at these colors! Deep brilliant blue, stone cliffs umber or ochre like calcified flesh, and wide glittering green.

The reason I came years ago.

And all those others followed.

These motorcyclists ride much too fast, she thinks, and they cut in much too close, and what a stink.

So, yes, how will it be to be in the house in the hills?

But at least it's not the house by the sea.

Love of her life.

But will you go see it?

SHE SWITCHES ON THE RADIO.

Crackling and then—

Help! I need somebody!

She switches it off.

Lively music, but need is a bore.

AFTER MONACO SHE FINDS THE WAY FROM THE CORNICHE DOWN the switchbacks to Rq and Cap M, an old loved route, all those summertime drives from Paris. Then past the cape toward Menton, along the beach a mile or two, into town, and the sharp left to the road that winds and twists for twenty minutes up to her second house. Time.

She parks, dust drifting, gets out, shakes hair, and stands hands on hips in the road. All around is the land she'd bought, that view, down over the seventy-two lemon trees and vines and far away to the shore, then back up to the shocking last Alp. And the house she built: arising from fieldstone, white and slim and mod.

Satchel over shoulder, typewriter under arm, she passes through the gate and climbs the narrow concrete steps to the white terrace. Palms, the trumpet flower grown so tall, her lounge chairs. The bridge over the garden to the guest room and kitchen. Glass wall of sliding doors to her study, her lounge.

But as she steps across the terrace to the glass, time slips: a piece of past floats up. There is Bado sitting in the sun in her lounge chair, smoking, brown hand shaking, turning to her with his gapped teeth and crawl of mustache.

Bado gone ten years.

She looks around the space, from the sliding louvers she'd made to screen terrace from road, over the black-tile sun box.

She turns back to the glass doors, slides them open—

The past can come back not just in images but smells

Oil paint, turpentine, fine

Her foot pauses a moment—then down the two block steps and she's in, once again in her studio-lounge. All the built-ins she'd made, desk and shelves, low sofa, trouser closet, pivoting drawers, louvers like gills all around.

Overhead: her ceiling eye.

She grips the lever and cranks—

And a crescent of clear blue sky appears.

How clever she was to make this!

But the sight of her hand against that slice of sky—

Some ossify

She sets satchel on dresser, places shirts in pivoting drawers, hangs trousers, puts typewriter and paper on desk. Then back out to the terrace and quickly down the concrete steps to the car for Louise's basket, and back up and over to the kitchen, out of breath now, to put away the sandwiches and soup.

To look at the kitchens she's designed this woman has never cooked a meal

Woman woman

Past also comes back in voices

She hurries back out the sliding door to the patio, over the bridge, down the other concrete steps on that side to look into the garden and up at the house so white against blue, cicada shrieks rising and falling in the fields. How to extend Time?

DUSK NOW, THE LIGHT GONE GREEN AND EARTH BREATHING, SKY open wide. Time for a little aperitif, she thinks. Ah yes, thoughtful Louise—a bottle of Pernod.

She sits in her curving S-chair, this slim old woman now slightly curved herself, and lets her eyes (though one's blind), ears (though a bit deaf), and nostrils (both splendid) absorb the evening, the smell of lavender and dung, far barks, flitting marks in the sky, swifts or bats. Lets it all float into her as she sits, legs crossed, milky liquid dancing in the glass in her hand, alone on a white terrace with a world circling around her, a vast tumbling landscape of vineyards and lemon trees and gorges and hills, stark sharp rock, towering ledge of land, distant hazy sea.

How fine, she thinks, to be a human animal porous to this world.

She sips, watches a crow soar, decides, why not, another. The cork-topped table muffles the clatter of the shaky hand that designed it thirty years ago.

The darkening sky is expansive, violet, with a sliver of yellow moon. Colors, she thinks: see them as they are alone and then side by side, how they're altered. As one is altered by anyone near, she herself never able to *be* herself with anyone near, brainless then. But alone, so free, thoughts pinwheel!

A reason not to let Pruny come.

Even if she thinks I'll be overcome back here.

I've survived it this long, after all.

Down over the fields and vineyards and gorge, past Menton, the other side of the cape: her house by the sea.

Someone no doubt in it right now.

The woman who got the house, down there now, getting up from one of Eileen's chairs, stepping out to the deck, smelling the fresh salt and hearing the clatter as waves rush through pebbles

Will not think this

Have done well for years.

Sordid history is what it is, she always says with a dry smile.

But will you go see it?

Pruny knows the history backward. Knows there's nothing to be done.

Except rage.

Eileen stands abruptly. Eat your sandwich, she thinks. Put dishes in sink. Pull trousers off, nightie on. Clean teeth.

Bluish moonlight, thin shadow, bare bony feet on tile.

Lights off. Lie still.

Living ghost.

2

SATURDAY, 21 AUGUST 1965

Le Grand made the connection from the Paris train an hour ago so should reach Cap M by seven. He's left projects in the office well in hand and the apartment closed up, so it's time for a holiday at last, once he gets through the Venice drawings and that tiresome interview. Already the end of August! Hands on knees, he peers through the train's scratched window and his own round glasses, obstinate behind their glint. He stares at the blue sea rolling by and feels the world he's made rolling in his wake: the early villas—those exquisite white machines; concrete church like a mollusk; ramped slabs for monks to live in; a city in sand; and all his photos and drawings and sculptures and words, shouted, printed, scrawled. And don't forget his paintings. But painting is one thing he does not do so well, and for this he forgives no one.

Le Grand. Despite the huge built world he's made, it's to a tiny cabin he goes, with tamarisk and cactuses and aloes on a narrow earthen terrace above the sea. His true home. More than home: the cabanon is his shell, he the squirting thing inside. He's felt this ever more the past months, everything growing a shade darker each day as he's retreated into his skull—ever more inward, into the dark, ancient man into a cave.

Or grave. He shrugs. The same.

The Venice hospital project will profit and suffer from this turn in his mind. Every patient will lie enclosed in a cell of walls, not even able to see the sky, just ghost of light through a slot. Architect must control the view always; architecture above all optical.

Hospital, cemetery

The train emerges from the tunnel at Monaco, rattles on the tracks between corniche and coast, slips back into the mountain: the land here is huge Alpine loaves of stone sliding into the sea, shapely but a torture to ride through. There's a retinal burn of sea glare before Le G is again in sooty dark tunnel, then a new sear of light. He puts a hand to his eyes until the train leaves the last tunnel and slows as it approaches Rq, passing eucalypts, vines, olive trees, lemons, a man trudging with a wheelbarrow of rocks.

Le G lifts his bag, grips the back of a seat, lurches down the aisle. Now the slow whine of brake, sigh of dying engine. Stillness. Doors crank open, and he steps from train to platform, into the hot smell of sleepers, tar, shit. Shifting the bag on his shoulder, he crosses the cracked concrete toward the path running alongside the tracks.

Warm pines, cypress, far sparkle of water, buzzing flies.

His ribs feel packed as he trudges, something stuck inside. Rats is what he said to Hindermeyer yesterday, rats rooting around.

Heartbeat's off, Hindermeyer had said. So no more pastis. Or morning swims. Or late nights working. And every day: the shots.

All right, all right.

Mostly: he must finish the Venice project with young Rebu,

Tino, then meet with that writer for his tedious questions, then finally have a holiday. Holy day, pure day, to do what he likes. Draw, paint. The impossible composition of women: how to fit three in a single plane. Puzzle he will finally get right.

He walks the path along the graveled tracks, past electrical lines and morning glories, hot air shimmering, until the path slips into the shade of sycamores and eucalypts. One set of narrow steps drops down to the cove, the next down to the white villa, but he walks on, toward his shed of holiday rooms, brightly painted and on stilts, the mural of his Modulor Man on the first to greet him—feet on earth, hand reaching toward sun. Joyous! Inside his jacket, inside his skin, Le G's nerves return the greeting.

Beyond the holiday rooms, another set of narrow steps down, this time to the fish place, and a few more paces and he's reached the small moment of ecstasy each time he arrives: the broad steps that sweep down from the path to his earthen terrace. His workshop with corrugated roof to the left—can almost pat its head as he passes—and to the right, amid carob and cactus, his cabin.

Breathe deeply, grow young, for the sea is the center of the world, his element since he first plunged into it, broken free of Switzerland. And this small place is the center of himself. *Mediterranean man!* He scuds down the last of the steps and over the path to the cabin, rough-hewn logs, mirrored shutters, palm-frond screen. Perfect: midway between cradle and coffin.

Inside, a smell of dry leaves and mouse, late sun falling in and glowing color where it strikes, golden yellow of the floorboards, glossy blue-and-yellow mural at the entry. Three paces and he's through the entry passage, where he drops his hat on a painted peg. Then turn and behold, the place entire: the cabin could be a sleeping compartment, ingeniously snug, made to the measure of man, this man. Narrow bed-platform from one wall, slim table projecting from another, shelves and drawers built into a third, red drape in the corner hiding the toilet. Insides of shutters he's painted with figures, sexy and voluptuous, red and yellow and blue.

This cabin: his greatest, smallest pleasure. At first glance rough, but no: exquisite.

A cabanon for you, my love. He'd slid a napkin with a sketch of the place toward Von a decade ago.

This?

There, look now, she almost appears in the dimness: her narrow white face, stark nose, fretful eyes, black hair bundled in a scarf. There, at the table, her silhouette as she sips a drink at dusk. And on the narrow bed, a curve of bones in the sheet.

His regret.

Not for making the place as he did, but for making her

No. She's resting, she rests now.

Up above the train tracks, up above the corniche, beyond the castle, in a tiny compound he designed for them both, inside a small cylinder marked with a cross, Von's a dry pool of ash.

And Le G is stricken again, again the awkward long-armed boy who first met her, precarious on large rude feet, and she a hearth angel, pots of fish stew steaming behind her.

After a moment, grunting, he drags himself back.

Miss her, yes. Now clear her gently away.

Look instead out the window, at the sea.

The sea he's not to swim in now.

Not enough that Von is gone: he's to have all life stripped away.

No. To hell. He'll swim and drink and work as he likes!

He shrugs off his jacket, drops it over a peg, unknots bow tie, pulls off shirt, trousers, saggy underpants, socks. In the center of the cabin he stands naked and damp, belly heavy. He rubs his arms against pale breasts, flesh slipping on flesh. Takes dirty painting pants from a peg and steps into them, legs trembling, straightens, ties rope around waist, puts hands on hips and becomes a man again, a large heavy man, the only life left in this cube of air.

WHEN IT'S NEARLY DARK, HE TAKES THE FAT ENVELOPE THAT'S BEEN waiting for him and steps through the small door between the cabin and old Rebu's fish place. There's a clatter of pans and voices, Rebu in a singlet by the bar. The old men nod and Le G heads to the patio, Rebu's dog behind him.

He's been waiting, Rebu says.

Good boy. Where's your son?

Hunting dinner.

A joke: young Rebu, Tino, as a child caught urchins for Von and stood between her knees, singing; her eyes flowed love toward the child but darkened when she turned back to her husband. *Madame begs me for children but how savor touching like that a girl you've married? Different rooms for different things, red and blue and yellow rooms, for whores and mothers and wives.*

Le G takes a seat on the terrace, drops on the table the envelope from that writer ridiculously named Piccolo. He waggles his fingers for the dog to trot over, catches its wet tongue and squeezes until the dog wriggles and presses a paw to his arm. Dropping it a heel of bread he gazes out to the shoreline. He strokes the dog's head, tender snout, whiskers, and silken lids, ear tips melting at his fingers. His own dog lies flat on the studio floor in Paris, athough his jawbone's here, an ornament on his desk. Still cherished.

Wine, says Rebu, and clunks a jar of dancing liquid on the table. Mussels?

Le G nods and puts both hands on the jar, the wine palest green, glass sweating as much as he. He pours, drinks, holds the cold tumbler to his forehead, and looks beneath the chill ache to the sea. The water is dulling silver now, tiny lights starting to appear along the bays and in yachts, brighter over toward Monaco.

Vonny, Von, from Monaco.

Ache in his head, ache in his ribs. Really feels as though something is stuck there

Drink.

A wet ring now on the envelope; may as well open it. A polite letter from Piccolo writing a (yet another) book about him. He'll be here tomorrow for some subtler questions, he says, so grateful for this time, et cetera, but meanwhile a packet of pages to check, bibliography, catalogue of images, chronology. Ah, god, from the start. Le G's birth and schooling, and just the dates and names give a stale breath of the gridwork town and clockmaking father and old apartment with its antimacassars. But his mother, sweet aerial mother, her golden piano, notes translated through her fingertips to air.

Drink, look to horizon, adjust eyes, turn a page.

Oh, all of it, his young-man travels, boots over the Alps, first seeing the liquid colors of Venice in 1910, white cubes of a monastery on rocks. *I am frantic to make and DO*, he wrote his mother, *my hands like dangling red paws and a tongue wild to plunge into everything!* Painting drawing design spurted from him, manifestos, a world he was going to build, rid this old world of macassary filth, make it radiant, new: ocean liner same as the Parthenon: ship and temple: form and light. Beauty only in function, air, light, and form, *A house is a machine to live in.*

I will especially appreciate, Piccolo has written, *any illumination you might give on the relationship between your seaside cabin and the jewel in the crown, the white villa, as I have a private theory—*

Le G pushes the papers aside, shoves glasses to forehead. A blur now before him, better, just deepening violet sky and pale glint of wine, and at last the smell of mussels. Garlic wine steam rises from a bowl floating toward him in the boy's hands, black shells jostling in hot pepper oil, split to bright flesh.

Tino, smiling, always nervous, even though he's properly a young man now, sometimes works in Le G's Paris office.

Bon appétit!

Le G is already eating, tongue parting a frill of plump orange.

Mother'll be over later for the injection, Tino says. And tomorrow—

We'll go over the Venice drawings. Then you can have them.

Have them?

To take to Amadeo.

Tino looks up. I'll take the project to Venice?

Le G drinks the hot salty juice from a shell and drops it back in the bowl. He opens another with a twist of fork, prongs the tender orange flesh, and pops it hot into his mouth.

Through with traveling, he says, and as he stares at the boy he thinks, I've said it, now it's true.

AFTER DINNER, HE WALKS IN THE DARK TO HIS WORKSHOP, SITS ON the whiskey crate, and unrolls the Venice hospital. A set of interlocking concrete slabs floating above black water, slabs resting upon pillars driven into the mud, cubes of darkness for the boatmen to row through. Slab after slab, each filled with rooms, each room with a bed in it, and on each bed, a black Modulor Man.

Still, here are the principles he developed in the twenties, principles that transformed the built world. Buildings on pilotis like thin legs, open plans, et cetera. Only the style is different now, for instead of being smooth and white, this manner is rough, raw, dark.

He inks in a tiny Modulor Man upon a bed. Soothing to ink like this, fill lines with black, and it keeps being not *hospital* but *cemetery*. Why should patients see out a window to life going on? No: lie on slabs and gaze through slits at the light, reflect on what's to come.

Pen down, he flexes his fingers, stares out at the blackness, at his own reflected face. Pushes the glasses up to his brow and rubs his eyes, then shifts the crate over to look at the old sketches of women on trace paper pinned to the wall.

How to get three in one plane. A compositional puzzle that has vexed him for decades. He places a fresh sheet of trace over the last one, shifts the woman lying slightly to the right, extends her knee just enough that its contour is shared by the breast of the other as she reaches from the floor . . . But then the form is too compacted, doesn't fill the plane properly.

He's drawn luscious armfuls of women ever since he was a boy, before he'd even seen one naked and could only imagine, so did, hard, imagine feeling a woman's plump bottom, feeling a breast full in his hand, feeling a nipple bend to his thumb. He'd look down at the paper beneath his damp palm where a figure had swelled to life and would himself swell beneath the table, want to eat or plunge into her. And when girls became real, his first days in Paris, *I want to plunge into everything*, he wrote, tongue in muddy roses, slaps and slippery flesh and sheets gritty beneath his knees and all of him concentrated in the eggplant muscle that was more his heart than what beat in his chest. That girl with red hair, the one with brown, the other with nipples like wilted dark blossoms but a bottom so fabulously fat in his hands, shoving himself in again and again until finally he exploded like stars. Then after sliding from one of the girls, he'd pull out his other favorite instrument, his pen, and arrange them—What I want is for you to lie like this—All three of us?—Yes, but you lift your knee, hands here, head here, and you your bottom up, knees apart, wider—and meanwhile Von his little shopgirl was tapping her foot at home, the clock of her mind revolving around him, Von his wife-to-be, but it was impossible to touch her like these girls, because of the different rooms for different things, red and blue and yellow rooms. If they mixed, if they could possibly mix, then there'd be clarity, an ideal—

A knock on the shack door, and his hand slaps to the table.

Yes?

A gray head peers in: old Rebu's wife, Marguerite.

He stands, suddenly courtly.

Sorry to come so late.

No matter.

Yes, she says. Heartbeat, we must take care.

Her eyes are clear, cheeks mottled, and she pulls from her apron pocket a small bag; from it, a vial and syringe. She draws liquid in, holds it to the lamplight, taps.

Best face forward, please, monsieur.

Dry old woman. He turns, unties the rope at his waist, lets his trousers drop, grunts as he bends, hands on the table.

A dab of icy wet on his rump, swift stab.

He winces, and knows this gives pleasure.

A big man to be hurt by such a small needle, she says, showing him its length. But she pats him on the shoulder before he gropes, knees creaking, for his puddled trousers.

Thank you. Another day of life shot into this old sack.

She laughs and leaves, and he watches as she moves from the light of the door into dark. He knots the rope at his waist and gazes for a moment at his belly, the soft folds. Then out at the black beyond the window.

Night sometimes soft and expansive, sometimes stark.

This ache in his ribs.

Heart. Heart.

He looks at the two bones on the sill, and picks up the little one. Often he just keeps it in his pocket. But sometimes he needs to hold it and rub it gently with his thumb.

Enough for tonight. He places a pebble on each corner of the drawing, brushes away eraser shreds. Steps out of the workshop to the cooling air. Leaves stir; far below, small waves break.

IN THE DARK, HE LIES GINGERLY ON THE NARROW BED, HIP PRESSING into a mat thin upon wood. He'd wanted this, a room like a cell, it soothes him, and the sound of waves soothes him, water rushing through pebbles, then calm, but merging with their rush and lull is a gentle beat beneath him, something not outside but in, more than just his heart, like something butting its head at his ribs, but enough now, breathe deeply, breathe.

Miles west along the coast, past Monaco and Nice but before Marseille, which once was Massilia and before that who knows, there the waves that roll in and roll in and endlessly roll in have carved not only cove after cove in the chalky cliffs but caves. One of these caves was once on dry land, but the sea has since poured in, and it's long been underwater; only divers can reach it.

Twenty thousand years ago, when the cave was still on land, the people who lived nearby would go in from time to time. They'd bring charcoal, shells, color they'd ground from umber or clay and smudged into paste with fat.

They might bow their heads at the entry, take a breath, step into the dimness. When their eyes found form in the dark, they would touch to find rock wall. Then be still and breathe softly, wait to feel what they might draw from the rock.

There, that smoothed knob with a runnel midway—like a girl's secret part: a boy might run his thumb up and down the slender runnel, take his charcoal and do it, too. And animals, the ones they knew, if they felt one hiding inside the rock, they would draw it out with charcoal or fingers, wher-

ever the rock gave a shape: here, a seal, there, an auk. This stone lump—a horse's haunch.

These people drew beautiful horses: clear black eyes and muzzles, flying manes drawn with combing fingers. Fingertips dipped into oily black, then run gently along stone.

After drawing, something else should be done, a kind of end, important. They'd drawn these creatures from the stone; now, themselves? Each person set a reed to their lips and pulled in black or red powder. Carefully each placed a hand on the rock, then blew—blew color between and around each finger, around the thumbs. Then gently pulled the hand back.

There.

3

SUNDAY

Back east around the coast to Monaco, past Le Grand's cabin, over the pines, eucalypts, and ancient olives, out to the tip of Cap M, in along the wide beach that curves beside Menton, then through town, with its seaside flats and balconies and bright cars and potted palms, and up the steep road along the gorge, up past the vineyards, to the white house with gangplanks rising from fieldstone: Eileen lies curled asleep.

Wake up, wake up, get up: *time!*

The usual disarray, but worse now as she both lurches from dream (a white dove folding its wings around a girl barefoot on the highway) and forgets where she is—then realizes, but thinks it's ten years earlier, so lurches in time, too.

She sits, rubs sand from her eyes, remembers that one eye does not see. Difficult; off-balancing at first, but she's grown used to it. She looks with the good eye to the bedside table for coffee.

Of course not. Louise is in St. T, Eileen is here alone, and it is not 1955 but 1965. She's alone in her house, which is no longer her house, up among the vineyards, morning light slanting through louvers, this house she built thirty years ago to get away from the house by the sea.

Overhead: her ceiling eye. She reaches up, thin arm with delicate old-lady skin, grasps the lever, turns, and opens a crescent of blue. Another turn and sunlight drops in as if this were the Pantheon, a cascade of light upon her thin face.

Some putrefy, others ossify

Her ceiling eye was always good, too, for letting out smoke. Propped on an elbow, she takes a cigarette from the bedside table, lights a match, draws, blows an arabesque that drifts through eclipse to sky.

Get up, make coffee. Wash. Button blouse, belt trousers, slip on shoes. Put on glasses (black lens helps with that eye). Get to work.

Then she's outside in the brilliant blue looking at the cliff like towering flesh stone, all the green. Brightness was exactly what she'd wanted when she came, to be soaked in light. She paces the length of the terrace and bridge to measure roughly; the old numbers will come back. To create an extension, separate quarters for living or working, as Graham said: is it better to run an extension over the public path (why she'd made that bridge) or make something new and strong in the garden, another bridge perhaps?

Don't want fussiness.

One bridge enough.

Would help if she had the old drawings. Oh if those dogs of soldiers, no not dogs love dogs oh little lost Domino, if those damned soldiers who moved in when she and Louise were forced to leave in '40 (resident alien!), if those soldiers who camped here and the looters behind them those four cold years she left the poor house abandoned, if they hadn't burned not just her tables and chairs but her drawings for heat—well. But she has them printed in her mind (good old mind) (sometimes) and is looking at it all again now, can overlay the recollected drawings on the actual place. Her hands are so shaky she can't draw quite as she once did, but loose sketching like this (back inside) will suggest what she sees.

Handwriting going to pot.

The shake came when she was small.

Just what were you afraid of?

Oh

Running down the dark halls of Brownswood from the shadows into her room panicked and quickly the lock

Eileen closes her good eye, adjusts her glasses, places both hands on the paper.

It is not, she knows, scientific to think that old fears can lead to an old lady's shake. But there are other truths beyond the scientific. Feelings leave traces in flesh.

In any case, she decides, the typewriter is excellent even if hands shake. Never mind the errors or when a word might end, just bang the carriage and carry the word to the next line.

Extending the line of the original kitchen but dro

pping to the level below seems to ~~be~~ me the most

Funny, she thinks: that Graham wants to extend Time.

Whereas I

Suddenly exhausted, she drops shoulders, lets chin fall to chest.

What an old lady. Enough, a glass of water. Go outside, soak your bones in sun. Lie in the beautiful black sun box you made, like a little black-tiled pool but no! Made for bathing in the sun upon soft sand. Roll up trousers, hell's bells, pull them off, there's no one to see.

But possibly the postman

No, he won't come up those steps.

She pulls off her trousers, drapes them over the edge of the black sun box, and there her legs are, shanky things, going faintly blue.

An amazement that she can be inside the same body for over eighty years, but almost none of this flesh is the same.

And yet all the past jostles inside it.

And here it comes now. Just touching the warm glossy tiles of the sun box, she is back at the house by the sea. Memories do live in flesh—oh, head, you can't stop this.

Because now the tiles have melted into something even earlier, the glossy blocks of her white screen, the one she showed at the Salon of '22.

There it is.

Tall folding screen of lacquered white blocks pivoting on brass rods. And there she stands beside it, young and tall with short black hair, black trouser suit, shy and proud, showing this gorgeous minimal thing, after her gloriously rich chairs and tables and lamps so nouveau for a time until they felt old—this was the first piece to be modern.

And there's Bado, dry hand reaching hers, stylish, slapdash, long legs, disheveled, hair stirring in his own breeze. Whiff of cigarette, bergamot, somehow off-kilter, face split in that grin, saying Hello hello, so honored to meet you, have followed you your work for some time, your chairs and tables the earlier screens and lamps where do I even start? Your elegant shop! And now this, look at this (finger gliding along a slick white brick). Modern!

His comical mustache and live eyes, you could feel clouds flowing across them.

Beautiful, he said, his fingers swiveling a lacquered brick, making a window to peer at her through.

And Le Grand was there as well, wasn't he, his boulder head, those glasses, and something lewd in that mouth as he appeared beside Bado, looking through the screen at her too.

Eileen opens her eye, lets light fall in, the distant voices of men in the vineyard, a dog barking, a truck working gears up the road.

The Salon of '22. Where this story began. Her white block screen and on the other side of the hall, beyond the scrolled and gilt and feathered things, Le G's white cube house on pilotis, slim legs. People glanced at it and then at her screen, as if she and Le G were a tribe, which was what excited Bado, wasn't it, this verge of a movement he could seize, now saying, Let me feature you in my magazine, do you know you're Modernism personified? You are. I mean it, don't laugh.

And here's Bado's face again, in her Paris flat, and had she painted the walls black yet or were they still dark blue? Bado in her fat Bibendum chair, crossed leg jogging as he laughed and drank, then her brushing by to get more drinks and he placed a warm palm on her hip, looked up at her with satyr eyes. Your only trouble, he said, is you're fatally aloof. But I'm not, I'm a tart, so we're perfect.

EILEEN WIPES HER MOUTH, GETS TO HER ELBOWS, FLOPS A LEG OVER the edge of the sun box, creaks herself up.

Hungry.

Must be a market open somewhere. Could surely manage simple things. Eggs, cheese, bread, olives, wine.

Soon she has trousers back on, hair combed, sunglasses to hide eye and because glamorous, still she is glamorous. Down the concrete steps to Totor 2, hot metal in sun, and decides to drive up to the old village first, must be a market somewhere, don't want to go all the way to Menton, don't want to go near the sea house.

Then up the switchbacks, jerking car into the tiniest space between rubble and rock, and she climbs up old stone steps to the central square, quiet and empty.

Hello? she calls to a man smoking in a corner. Can you tell me, where's the market?

What?

The market, groceries.

A slow exhalation; a peer through smoke.

It's Sunday.

So, gingerly back down the steps, into the car, down the switchbacks, past the gorge, twenty minutes to Menton. She finds the covered market by the port, smell of sea. Same. Shut. But there at last is a stand open on the street, a girl in a short flowered green shift.

You're open! Eileen sings. One of those cheeses and a quart of cherries and eggs and a loaf. And wine?

Ah, she thinks, back in the car. No going to the dogs today. How about a picnic? On the beach?

She drives slowly, ignores the honking. Looks toward the beach, the bikinis.

Would she have worn one?

Yes.

Would've designed one if she'd designed clothes.

But would've been too ladyish.

Wanted to be one of the architect boys.

While having nothing to do with them.

It's time you built a house, Bado had said. You know it, don't you? She hears it now, sees his eyes, his grin.

But already it's perilous, as she drives along the broad beach, waves crashing on pebbles, rushing back, and the salt smell, and already she sees where the beach curves out and becomes Cap M, oh too close already. There's the flat she rented to work in four decades ago, drawings and models all over the floor, Bado in Paris waiting for word on how it was coming, her house by the sea, genius experiment, masterpiece, love, the thing they'd decided she must do, and she turns to drive away from the coast and back up to Time, but when she reaches the train track, lights flash bells clang and down comes the bar. So she has to wait as the train rattles near. And there's the hot sweet stink of sleepers and tar, and it's that day in '25 when she first came down here looking.

Close your eyes, no choice.

AND THERE YOU WERE—IT WAS SO LONG AGO THAT THE TALL GIRL she sees in her mind really feels like someone else—there you were walking along the train tracks, in the glaring light. Tall and strong! look at you! under a broad hat tapping sleepers on the tracks with a stick as you walked, smelling sea and pine, and the glittering water, sweat sliding into the corners of your mouth, can taste it. Hand over eyes, boots hot, looking for the spot, had to be on stone almost in the sea, and you were so excited, just had to find the spot at a price you could manage and this was the time, with your mother just gone. You'd been making models, studying spaces that fit the body, train compartments, ocean liner berths, where a bed folds out to cover the seat and a table slides from the wall, you'd been yearning to design a house that was intimate and modern but not a machine. But always fears (it'll collapse). Then Bado had come along so go-go and said, The technicalities of building psshhh you'll get that in no time I'll help you.

And as you did think things through you gathered resources, and with the money from Mum and the chairs rugs screens et cetera you finally sold when you closed your shop keeping just a few things in storage you decided yes, bank everything on this, because if not now, when you're forty, when?

You knew the spot at once. On the edge of a cove of pebbled beach, that slab of rock. Look at you clambering down, cutting your thumb, blood in your mouth, the water ravishing in green white rings by your boots. Squinting up at the sky, seeing the space in the air where it would be: like a slim white yacht on the rock.

Too close to the water, Bado said when you told him.

No we can do it.

The rock's so difficult, he said.

But we can screw it into the rock, a steel staircase

Spiral?

Yes! That'll fix it into the rock, and the house will grow from the spiral the way the sun moves

Then at the town hall you learnt that an Irishwoman could not own land on the coast. Simpler to buy it in Bado's name.

So

Foolish (love) but you were rash and excited and wanted to go go, and then the delirium of making. Three years! Teaching self everything! Savant autodidact call it what you like you were already famous in mechanics of chairs and drawers and so on, not so different, you always found your way to make them.

Yes sitting on the floor of the flat in Menton cutting cardboard to make a model of the slab following contours from geological maps cutting squares of Perspex and arranging, rearranging, paper rolled out across the parquet floor, nights eating sandwiches and drinking bottles of beer while the seagulls cried dinosaur cries. Plotting how the sun moved, and waves and tides, and how you and Bado moved, what your bodies did each day, each step, and letting the house grow around this, squinting to see how Bado would lean to open a blind or slouch in slippers with coffee or reach to a doorknob for a tie. And you'd follow Louise throughout the apartment, having her tape chalk to her shoes to leave on the floor her daily transits as she opened shutters, made tea, washed linens, hung them, dusted, cooked, switched on lamps.

To see how the house could be the living shell of those inside, formed by them. House like a mollusk. Made of liquid stone. Windows and shutters slid along tracks to let in sun and breeze or block them, windows not the mean slits Le G liked but membranes, *organic*, and the spiral staircase like the whorl of a whelk, connecting house to ground and sky—

When you brought a model to Bado in Paris he peered, big eye through a tiny ribbon of windows, and said, Wonderful, but another bedroom so we can have clients stay, it'll be a show house of our work.

Our work, you thought, ha, but didn't really mind, and found a mason who'd learn concrete and a carpenter who'd learn Bakelite, and ordered sand and cement and boarding for casts, and steel and glass and tiling, rubbing your eyes calling out numbers in the sun, dusty and hot and blistered, baking as you checked and changed and changed again, throwing yourself into the sea to relax, oh those luscious moments, swimming the length of the cove.

And finally! Oh but it hurts to remember this, hurts but is so sweet too, the first time really coming to the house.

Bado had seen it only a handful of times as it rose from the rocks, seen it and made a suggestion or two, glanced at the drawings and drawn a line, erased one. Then the weekend you and he drove down from Paris, parked at the station, walked along the path by the pines and morning glories and oleanders, down the narrow dark steps, through the gate, and you could almost see water reflecting, dancing, on that smooth white concrete skin. Reached the tiled entryway and the question of the doors, *Enter slowly*: your first little joke! And Bado knew which door of course but paused for fun, nearly turned left toward the kitchen but spun on a toe and stepped right, and then you were in, letting him go first, the heat of him you could feel through his jacket in the curving red entryway that made you enter especially slowly, as if sliding into a whelk, until you were truly inside—standing on the pale tiles before the wide slash of sea. Then both of you inspecting everything—did the blinds turn out right? And the screen over here, and how about the shelves that pull down? The little mirror? So small but perfect. And you watched his handsome brown feet tread tiles you laid for him, his satyr face grinning in that mirror you made him, his stained hand spinning open a drawer you'd made him, and the pleasure of it. Then the heart of the place, the spiral steps, the two of you hurrying practically on top of each other down them round and round then pausing dizzy slumped together to look up, up to the sky moving slowly through the glass nautilus roof. And the way he gazed at you then: the look that sees you and the extraordinary thing you've made, and you are gold, you are gold. Then you let him, silly but oh, smash a champagne bottle on the house's flank, christened! Then pull out a fresh one of course to pop pour and toast, the two of you standing in the early evening light, canvas awnings all tied back, so you could gaze at the gleaming water rolling forward, at the huge clouds drifting above, and truly you *were* on an ocean liner, you and Bado, and you thought, Sail on and on and on.

STOP.

In the car, dry old hands on the wheel, staring blank
Train rattles by rattles by rattles
Is gone.

4

SUNDAY

Le Grand stands in the center of the cabin, stretches his arms and swings them in the space that fits so comfortably, as he was himself the measure. Bends to touch floor and up and down again and up; all his life is rigor, vigor. Year after year in Paris he rose in their lofty flat at six, slapped to the floor for push-ups, squats, and jumping jacks, had coffee and a pleasurable shit, brought Von her coffee, and then his greatest delight: going upstairs to his studio to paint and think before driving to the office, preposterously, perfectly, in a former convent. Now in this old body in the cabanon, it's a modest version of that grand routine. No jumping jacks, but yes squats.

Interesting how the column of air he occupies as he squats holds the smell the odor no *stink* of his body as down his head and nose go. *Le G is entirely masculine, nothing feminine about him.* Forget who wrote it or where (India? journalist maybe in India?) but he'd liked it enough to cite in one of his decade books, that volume of his *oeuvre complète.*

Doing this regimen, squatting deep, is when he most feels the stitches around his thigh, the pull. But the slight pain now jolts to mind the dream last night: of expelling from his body something alive, like birthing, good lord, a cat?

Regimen: make body strain. While brain is still loose from sleep, strange images and ideas still lurk within to be caught and used in painting. Squat, rise, arms out. Squat. Yes a cat and he can see it if he lowers his eyelids in dimness (shutters not yet open). A big cat ripping out of him, rank wet smell and tearing as somehow he birthed it, looking down at bloody slop and fur between his legs, how could he dream such a thing?

But, he thinks as he gets to his knees, lowers slick belly and breasts to the floor, presses palms upon the dirty yellow wood for a push-up, let's move past the humiliation of having a feminine dream and examine how I could possibly dream a thing I couldn't feel, with absolutely no knowledge to inform the feeling. Primal streams, ancient currents, they flow through me, he thinks, I have access to the ancient and raw, yes, especially when I sleep but now too when I concentrate on resurrecting what the uncivilized mind will do when let loose at night.

Pushing, grunting, knees slipping on wood

No sense to this dream yet.

Well, meaning will come, but now must get on with things, because Piccolo is coming at ten, and Le G wants to be rid of him as soon as possible so he can get done with Venice too and finally have his holiday. Already the end of August! And being so hemmed in, the morning and evening shots (Madame R will be over in a minute) and the writer and no swim and then Tino and not enough pastis, it's no wonder he dreams of birthing a wild cat, surely it's himself, of course it is, his own self caged when what he needs is

Le G is entirely masculine, nothing feminine about him.

Enough. Hand to the shutter, pulls it open to a square of blue, the Mediterranean light flaring in his eyes.

Ah.

And coffee! Kind Madame R has placed coffee outside the door. He hurries feet into the holes of pants, ties rope around waist, steps out to the sun, and lifts the small bowl of steaming froth.

Standing here in the silty soil, by the tamarisk, soft lush white petals of yucca fallen by his toe, spike of palm frond at his shoulder, platelike thorny cactus, sun soaking his face, looking out at the sea—

Mediterranean man!

AN HOUR LATER, HE WALKS OVER TO HIS WORKSHOP, DRAGS THE table and whiskey crate outside. One swoop, he thinks. Answer Piccolo's damned questions and be quick with the man himself.

When the writer appears at the top of the wide concrete steps, Le G thinks, Exactly as I'd expect. Too much mustache, tight striped pants! Little picholine eyes.

An honor, the man's saying as he trots down the steps.

Yes, says Le G, and points to the crate. You sit here and ask, and I will expound, and with luck you will capture my words and this will be done quickly.

The pants are too tight for a low crate but the writer manages and pulls out his notebook.

You won't sit too?

I think better standing. Start!

Well as I said in my letter, I'm most interested in any illumination you would be so kind as to give on your cabanon here, particularly how you chose this location. This modest property—Piccolo says, looking around at the actual place, the tamarisk and carob and pines and yuccas—the small log building. It's, as you know, surprising for an architect of your

Strange question, thinks Le G, because how does anyone choose a location?

Heart and money and opportunity, he says aloud, and I've always said, *Three skinny pine trees and four square meters of sand*, I've said it and sung it so really I preowned this place before I ever saw it.

Piccolo bends over the page to write, although how can he see through that mustache. But even as he gazes at the man, Le Grand begins to wonder. When did he in fact first come down here to Cap M, how did he come to this stretch of coast? He remembers instead another beach, an Atlantic beach with soft dunes and yellow flowers stitching through them, himself with men drinking and singing into the darkness over the waves: *Three skinny pine trees and four square meters of sand!*

In fact it was after this that he'd come here. Even *because* of this that he'd come here. Because one of the men, the ringleader, possibly? had been yes that silly Romanian, that gypsy, Dodo, Bodo, no, Bado, who always strode forward leering putting out his hand. That's right, an invitation to visit the Blue Coast to see Bado's new

So the phrase again, Piccolo says, the song you sang: Three skinny pine trees?

And four square meters of sand. Yes. Next question.

Well: of course a seaside house makes perfect sense, doesn't it, as the ocean liner aesthetic has always been yours.

Le Grand shrugs. This is not a question, he says. Everyone knows my early manifestos about the machine aesthetic, how a designer needs the mind of an engineer, how I set images of ships and portholes alongside Parthenon columns, shocking, yet they're equally functional, efficient, elegant—

Le G waits as the man scribbles, looking over his dark head out to sea, and wants to be in it, damn it.

So, he says now, note this firmly. An image of the Parthenon dropped into my mind when I was still battling just to be heard anywhere, walking down a wet Paris street one day, disgusted, who wouldn't be, disgusted with old Europe and its old engorged houses. Even before I ever said, *A house is a machine to live in*, just as I was getting to that idea, there dropped into my mind the image: white bones of an ancient temple against a blue sky, immaculate and rational: the Parthenon like an ocean liner.

As clear as that? asks Piccolo.

Yes.

A gift!

Yes, Le G thinks. There was a logic in the image appearing as it did. Everything had a kaleidoscopic order in his head, and it was up to him to perceive it and then up to others to follow.

Next question, he says.

The dramatic shift in your work from Purist, from the exquisite white villas to structures that are rough and course, the *béton brut*: that is, from whiteness and purity to the primitive and brutal: could you elaborate on what inner transitions occurred in your mind?

Le Grand stares.

Or perhaps the transitions were external and caused by the times themselves?

Does this person really imagine, Le G thinks, that the movements in an artist's mind can be so easily explained? He jabs fists at hips, looks (sailor) out to sea. Because that transition did happen. Something to do with, something to do with coming here. Sunlight, sea, rocks, and air! They seep into his skin whenever he's here, just as he seeps into those elements. Bare feet on pebbles or pine needles, arm reaching to the sun! His Modulor Man had begun stirring inside him two decades ago and became the great clarifying stroke: a graphic expression of man's profound unity with nature. All he's done since that point has been an ever firmer striding into the shaggy and raw. His house for the doctor in Argentina with a tree growing through its floors. His hulking apartment complex down the coast, midway between animal and city, blood vessels and intestines running through columnar legs, its skin concrete imprinted by the living patterns of trees.

How did this transformation actually happen?

Piccolo looks at him, pen waggling in his fingers.

a total transformation, Le G hears in his mind.

total transformation throughout

But those were his own words, in an *oeuvre complète*, describing what? Describing something he'd done, yes, that had effected a total change throughout a space, and it was yes a white space a pure space that had badly needed this transformation, needed to be less sterile less frigid, that's the word, frigid. So possibly yes if he's interested in his own transitions, his own developments, his *oeuvre complète* as architect (he is), then peering into that moment of total-transformation-throughout could be illuminating.

And odd, he thinks, walking away from Piccolo and around the workshop to inspect a yucca's white blossoms, realizing only now how fantastically loud the cicadas are, sawing away invisibly in the pine trees, you never realize until all at once you think, My god that racket rising and falling and pushing my blood pressure with it; how odd that in one's aesthetics and world vision one swings between ends of a spectrum, first the white and pure and smooth and then repelled by that and lusting for crust and bristle, blood. Because it's true that he moved from one end to the other and with a violence.

Was it perhaps the War? calls out Piccolo. It seems that

The War? says Le G. He stops, presses a palm against a plank of his workshop. What on earth would the War have to do with my inner transformations?

Then? Something inner, a private mechanism—?

Le G comes back around and looks over the writer's shoulder to his notes, pinecone and rock holding the edges of the page in the warm breeze (small bone is safe in his pocket, his thumb tenderly rubbing it, because no one else knows anything about his private self, loving self, and this little bone still feels like *home*, like Von. The smell of roasted garlic filling the flat and pastis already poured, Von, warm yellow center of his heart, sacred spirit of the domestic, unlike the blue the red the mother the whores, the glimpse still inside his eyes of Von climbing the block steps of their apartment in Paris to the roof every morning, because of the sparrows, she knew each one, she fed them. Von with her black hair and thin bird nose and hands scattering dry seed. Up the white steps, he could see her hands flung open to the sky—Von was the calm place from which everything worthy he has ever done flowed, and here he is now having to soldier on alone and who would ever ask any of this? No one; he is an octopus beaten on rock).

Piccolo coughs.

I ask about this transition in your work, he says, because the seaside villa and cabanon seem to embrace both your early pure and late *brut* facets, so I wonder whether this enclave by the sea is in fact a compact expression of your *oeuvre complète*?

All of this my *oeuvre complète*?

And suddenly Le G senses himself and this place in which he stands at a telescopic distance: half naked with glasses shoved up cynical forehead, standing on an earthen terrace built by men three thousand years ago and planted with olives and vines then abandoned and now planted with tamarisk, yuccas, and cactuses, and given new articulation via his workshop at one end and cabin at the other, then beyond the cabin the fish place, and beyond that the shed of holiday rooms, and below them all that white villa, slender, silent, alone.

All of this my *oeuvre complète*?

But wasn't, he begins to realize, the villa here first?

LE GRAND WILL KNOW THIS WHEN HE MAKES AN EFFORT. BUT HE will not make that effort in the presence of Piccolo, who is already packing up his papers and nodding and looking not nearly as happy as he'd hoped. No, making that effort is not what Le G wants to do. If he did, he might begin to remember more, if he kept boldly thrusting that searchlight into his cave. He would begin to recognize that the writer has it wrong about the villa, thinking that it is really part of Le G at all. He will remember more clearly: back in the twenties holidaying with a mob of men, among them that Bado, who for a time was so useful and published everything Le G wrote in that magazine of his, all his manifestos, Le G will remember when he first drove singing from Paris to a beach house in Arcachon, and there he drank and smoked and crashed into the sea, stared at the sky, waved his arms in the dark and conducted the stars; this was when he first learnt to conduct his arms and legs in water, to master that element, *swim*, throwing himself ecstatic into the luscious medium that has ever since parted for and enveloped him.

And he'll remember: what Bado said he was doing on the Blue Coast, the Mediterranean coast, on a glorious sliver of land, building a glorious house, a new experiment in Modernism that questioned with perfect delicacy Le G's own principles, and he knew Le G would want to see it (leering gypsy), and how this planted in Le G a sharp seed of irritation: that this shabby shadow of a man might dare imagine what he'd want to see, to say nothing of his actually building a glorious house on the coast, that this oily shadow of a gypsy should waltz into a villa on the sea and one made not only in Le G's own style but an experiment and *critique* of his work.

Maybe he'll remember: driving back from Arcachon, green Fiat muscling the roads, still seeing the soft dunes and yellow immortelles, still feeling the salt air and salt water on his skin, irritation growing into something else, and shouting angrily, *Three skinny pine trees and four square meters of sand!*

And then he might recall too how it felt when he happened to see pictures of this villa of Bado's alongside pictures of his own Villa S: photos of his lovely villa standing on its slim white legs on the grass outside Paris, right next to pictures of Bado's villa standing on its slim white legs by the sea. How this made him pause, lower his glasses to look. How irkingly smart, his own principles but not, how was that possible?

Not possible that Bado could have made this. Just not. Must be someone else involved. Yes, of course, Bado had a partner, of course he did—but what—a woman? And her name: slowly with the name came a figure. Lived near his office in Paris, that's right, tall, fair, striding walk, boots. Had a shop. Yes, he'd walked by it, on the Rue du F. Black, gold, elegant, caught his eye—and the chairs and so on inside: startling, something like, something like, well. What he'd been getting his own office to try. Dressed halfway between woman and boy, jacket belted hard at waist, she had some history didn't she with that singer, that actress, she was ah *that* kind. But she couldn't be, not if partnered with this fool Bado. What?

And sooner or later Le G will remember how he ran into grinning Bado on the street and said, All right then, why not, I'll come have a look at your little place.

And when he went, there it was, amid the rocks and pines and cactuses and sea, his sea, there it was, this alarmingly elegant, intelligent place, and there she was, standing at the entry, tall, pale eyes wide apart, little mysterious smile.

And he'll remember walking past lemon trees toward the house, toward her, and how she turned her body just enough for him to see the first teasing hint, those words stenciled on the wall. *Enter slowly.* And her small smile as she watched him consider them.

So which is it, mademoiselle, he murmured. Warning? Or invitation?

No, she said after a moment, after—what?—sizing him up. No, entering a house should be like entering a mouth, she said. Slowly, then once inside, feel it close around you, safe.

And all he could do was look at her and say *Really!*

Already he could see just inside the house, see and nearly touch a smooth, curving red wall within, and glimpse what lay beyond.

And as she moved beside him, silky trousers, silky blouse, she did not say much but what she did:

We believe in the sensual

But the senses will atrophy in this machine age

So we see a house as a shell

Really not—those eyes glancing—*a machine.*

And oh the beauty of her and of house, outrage of her and of house, rooted in him—as he moved through this place she somehow had made for herself and that fool—a tangle, a tangle of something.

Maybe he will start to remember this, and remembering can happen all over the body, not just in the head but in the ribs and over the skin, with its stitches and scars. His body might do the remembering, dig into the murkiest regions. And from there push up things he's forgotten, or decided aren't true, or decided are true, even though they are not.

In the cove, waves rush through, wash through pebbles, are pulled back to sea, rush through pebbles again, and this happens today and has happened for millennia. Over time, the waves have carved coves. This sea, the Ligurian Sea, now curves a mile more deeply into land than when people lived here nine thousand years ago, people who combed the pebble cove for cockles, white or brown, sometimes striped, ribbed. They gathered the cockles, roasted them, pried apart the curved plump shells, ate the delicate hot flesh. Cockle: Cardium edulis*: edible heart. Also called heart mussel. These people saved the shapeliest shells. Because pleasing? And when they fashioned pots, they'd take a shell and gingerly press it into the soft moist clay. Sometimes, carefully, they'd press just the edge, leaving a curved row of teeth; sometimes they'd press fingertips inside the shell and roll, leaving a small fan of ridges.* There.

5

MONDAY

Today, Eileen thinks as she turns from the terrace, fields, and trumpet flowers with tender poisonous flesh and steps back to the workroom, today you stay in the now.

And if you think about anything other than the project, only thoughts that wander not down to the coast but out to the world.

For instance, let's have a look at the newspaper.

She goes quickly back outside and down the concrete steps, finds the paper tucked between bars of the gate, takes it, notes that the mailbox is full so yes of course she'll be considerate, collect the envelopes and magazines, bring it all upstairs.

All right. Now a look at the paper.

A conference on the population explosion.

About time.

Well, I did my bit.

not a child among us and plenty of liaisons I imagine but no child

Just draw.

Lines flow from her hand, clear strong lines moving over the large sheet of paper, and one benefit to half blindness, she thinks, is all this freedom, big swoops.

Let's turn on the radio.

What's new, pussycat?

A growling voice, or no, sounds somehow like fuel. And is this the man, she thinks, to whom women throw their panties?

Pussycat, pussycat, I love

Drawing, sheets of paper and fat marker strokes (shaky) but it feels good, she loves everything she can do with her hands, although it's true the years of lacquer work were harsh. She was the only one doing such a thing, the only European lady anyway, once she'd gotten taught by Seizo, and oh, she thinks, I miss Seizo. Hard work. Skin just about peeled off. For every layer of lacquer (the minerals) another layer of skin, hands crimson.

Which Bado remarked upon when she first touched him (there), and not having used her hand for that (much) she hoped it'd come naturally, imagine being over forty (Pruny's age now!) and this being semi-new, but she seemed to be doing all right until he said, Your hand's a bit rough isn't it, grinning. No no don't stop I like it don't stop like a cat's tongue ah

Had a cat's tongue on you really? Here?

Just imagining, don't stop

Pussycat pussycat I love

And funny how drawing, so soothing, methodical, with even the silliest music on, sets the mind wandering, from one thought to another that must be connected somehow because yes of course from Bado and pussycat she's wandered to Damia, can hear her voice, her putting on a purr, *My little cat is hungry*, sweet mixed-up Damia, E can feel her thin ribs in her own arms even as she draws, can smell her smoky hair after a night onstage and oh whatever she'd do afterward she always would do something come home shoes fumbling off at dawn, the sootiness of her black dresses, glamorous shabby chanteuse dresses. But E did love her and yes she'd feed Damia's little cat, she'd put her cat tongue to Damia's little cat and feel Damia's slick belly, her tender hair, but now as E draws, Damia's skin and secret hair meld with the other that was often in the room, nervily in the room, Damia's actual cat, the big one, the panther, so many of those tricky ladies sauntered about Paris with big cats on jeweled leashes those days. What a thing to do! Because sexy? Powerful? Unnerving? Unkind to poor cats because it never could last, now could it. One bores. Ah Damia. Yes did love her but there's always the end it seems especially with someone like her, younger and too glamorous and seducible, whispers and little shades of trouble in her dark eyes, but mostly too generous with love. Yes just like Bado, the two of them so alike, naturally E would find them sliding over each other in her thoughts now, their smokiness, vagabond eyes dimming in pleasure, big broken smiles, what she'd loved about them both so pleasable so generous

Although that yes was the problem. Too generous with others, both of them, each with a parade of women sooner or later, people like that always need others and how humiliating it became the women Damia would skulk about with and the women he started bringing to the house by the sea to entertain the big men but

She tears away a sheet of paper now and stands, brushes off trousers, shakes one leg and the other, and wonders, Is it this place that dredges up all the past?

She steps (creaky) up the two steps, shoves open the sliding glass door (needs oil), steps out into the hot air, and decides that yes it is the place that brings back the time because all of it is inside her, swarming, figments like a Bosch. Or like that ancient mural in Mexico, the tiny blue figures spouting from a volcano, paradise and pain.

Oh, let's just stand out on the terrace again for a breath of air, the deep blue overhead, Alps still rearing up all the way down here, and who even knew about continental plates sliding into each other, casting up mountains! And the greens the browns oh words useless, fling them away.

I can love things I've always loved, she thinks. It's people (too shifty) to whom one should not attach feelings.

Except for some people like Louise and Pruny, in fact I'd better write Pruny, quickly before the postman comes, might not have come yet today, and then she'll have the letter tomorrow, as I can't call long-distance here, but maybe she'll remember to call. She did say she'd call, I wish she would.

Although she'll harass me

Bossy lately

What does she think I can do at this point?

She knows there's nothing.

But old, old rage.

Back inside, blinded, Eileen lurches down the two steps over the tiles safely back plop to the desk.

Typewriter. Bang bang

P dearest, I know I'm a bother but could you possibly see if they've taken care of the vines yet? At my age I know it's absurd to have a property like this to worry about but nevertheless there it is and it does need worrying until I can sell it. Thank you ~~by~~ my darling. Everything getting along well here as I think I ~~cabn~~ can see a way to extend Time (joke) without creating a second bridge, too fussy, and I must say that the more I work on this the ~~mn~~ore I hope that GS will take this to heart and actually do it. A commis-

sion, imagine, at my age. While here trying not to think about other matters the past the other place but you know this can be hard espeiccially for a lady like myself of frail mind ha ha

Well that's done. And while we're sitting here feeling otherwise blank about designing at the moment, but it will pass, while we're sitting here at this trusty machine the typewriter (not a machine to live in) (that a critic actually said Pruny's paintings are *a machine for seeing*, to drag out that old idea of his and stick it on her) let's bang out a letter that's overdue. Poor Steven: let's write him. So few friends still walking the earth! Steven, Kate, Natalie, Romaine, though scarcely any of them to be seen now, just written or maybe telephoned, and funny how one can float through bodies of people in one's life, feel them so close for years but then bit by bit they're gone like old clothes; Steven the oldest one left, from way back in the art-school days those first years in Paris, all the painting girls and poetry boys, the boys so tragic, but then Jessie in her boy costume and oh I was fond of her and that game, gallivanting about with her in a top hat and jacket and silly mascara mustache, and poor little Henry, the one Mum wanted me to marry, what a forehead, and he was awfully lucky not to marry me, what a mistake that would have been, because truly as we've now seen: I drift along best alone.

S, my dear (piteous lamenting S!), *as for love whether we think of the spiritual or the carnal side of the species, as you pair them, especially at our late age, I must say that I've found it on the whole rather less than satisfactory and have been glad to be done with it. Brotherly or sisterly love, though, is another matter. And the love I've had for the tortoise and a good number of cats and dogs. And of course Pruny. You speak of the potential ecstasy of merging into the infinite. But why conflate ecstasy with any kind of merging, when ecstasy is a stepping out of self?*

To step out of self! She pictures it, foot stepping out of her skin into air. Like hatching. Whereas trying to merge with another, imagining that the man or woman, the *being*, the *being* you hold in your arms, your mouth softly pressed upon, your eyes leaking into: foolish to think you're ever anything but alone.

Anyway. Let's get ourselves outside, for heaven's sake, put the letters in the box, head out with measuring tape, get something done. Something rough yet feasible is what you ought to finish now so that we can see how we could extend the house not by adding another bridge but by dropping a level below the kitchen to add another set of rooms opening onto the garden. Will need to excavate to establish grade but it would feel separate and private, like at the house by the sea where you had, yes, true, that's where this is coming from, another house that drops grade, where you had the extra bedroom set below the main one, that bedroom also private with a door looking out to the black sun box and sea and reached by the spiral stair, the spiral screwing the house into rock

ah how you merge the spiritual the sensual have I told you mademoiselle

No.

how for me you merge

Oh, can't stop this.

Close eyes. Surrender.

Because here it all starts to come again. Here is Bado running down the spiral steps once the house by the sea was done, clutching the first magazine (after his own) that showed the house, as she lay in that first sun box.

Look! he cried. A full spread. Nothing but praise! And look, we're in the same article as Le Grand. His Villa S. Just the two of us. Our two houses. Now we're linked, he said.

She laughed at Bado's crush but said, Show me, show me, and

took the journal, and yes it was thrilling to see her house, her first house, like this. Autodidact, she thought, idiot savant, and first house splash you're a star!

A fresh mark for Modernism, moving from the machine aesthetic beyond to the rationally sensual. What an explosion onto the scene by this pair

Yes *this pair* as she'd named the house for the two of them, hadn't she, her initials wrapping round Bado's, and of course they called it their house, having come up with the idea together. Bado was the front man, after all, and first published the house in his own magazine, after all, and was the one first to convince her to build, after all, and yes he had a number of useful ideas and helped her with countless technicalities, so yes of course it *was* a partnership, so yes, equal billing.

She bought another copy of the journal and sliced out the spread, the photos and drawings of Le G's Villa S, with its fine white legs standing upon grass and hers with its fine white legs upon rock. She studied his plans, his ramp but her spiral; his hard-framed view but her windows like membranes letting everything in; his machine, her shell. She pasted the pages into her *cahiers*, her private record of everything that mattered.

And how long after, two months? and the man himself was coming. The first summer she'd spend in the house, having driven down from Paris in Totor with Louise, Bado coming down a day or two later, and when he did he was bursting.

I ran into him on the street, Bado said. He's gotten married, her name's Von, he's been living with her secretly for years, she's from Monaco, used to be a model or shopgirl or something, and he's been asked to do a floating refuge in the Seine and a sea-side house and he's obsessed with houses by water and is dying to visit ours. Of course he's seen the article. He's driving down next month to meet Von's family, so I said absolutely, yes, please come.

So, then! Little to do to prepare, everything still so new, not even grime in the caulking yet. Oil a hinge, rub the windows, smooth the sand in the sun box.

On the day itself, at a rattle at the gate, Bado in sailor stripes pranced up the steps, and there was Le G's boulder head and striding legs, his little wife with smudged eyes behind him. Hellos on the path outside the house, Bado darting about, Von's glovelike hand in Eileen's. Then Le G stood beside her with those glinting glasses and a look of being amazed or affronted.

What a pleasure, mademoiselle, he said, taking her hand, and she felt something come off him, a steam.

Then he turned to the house, and he had a way of looking that established the scene to be looked at, so they all stood back to look too.

Then the *Enter slowly*, and the whelklike passage, him running a finger along the smooth red curve, giving her some sort of look, then all of them stepping through to the gleam of floor and splash of sky and sea

Ah!

They followed the great man as he strode about, lifting his glasses to note columns, touching, craning, crouching to look. The drawers and tables that swung from walls, the shutters that opened or slid away so the room closed or dissolved, they had found a way to make a room boundless, and was it true these shutters were patented, Bado?

Then down the spiral staircase, pausing to lean back and admire its glass nautilus roof, and out to the lower terrace.

So many surprises, he said, peering at the sun box. To deter mosquitoes, you say? Sand rather than water. Made for a man my size! And he stretched out his arms and stepped in.

Then into the main bedroom and bathroom, stroking the fur on the bed, the nickel, the glass, murmuring, So much sensual material.

Yes, she said, because in this machine age you know the senses

Yes?

Will atrophy

Will they, he said, looking at her, then Bado.

Finally he'd been down and up the spiral staircase twice, and now stood again at the broad ribbon window, light turning his form to shadow. He stretched out his arms, fingertips wide.

What could one possibly say, he said, but that one is thoroughly amazed.

Then Bado bubbling, pouring champagne, Von already sipping. But Le G stood still. His gaze moved again over the rich spare spaces, out to sea, and back to Bado. Then rested upon Eileen.

HAPPY BADO AFTER THIS! HE SPUN EILEEN, KISSED HER, WAS THE pearl in the oyster, she'd made the shell herself. And how hopeful she was, for soon she'd be called to make new houses, because now they'd caught Le G's interest oh more would come. Weekend parties now at the house by the sea, because this was what mattered, Bado said, this social net they were making.

Then Bado brandishing another magazine. Look!

A neat little piece about Maison Bado.

The illustrations are excellent, he said. I let them have the plans and a few images but didn't know if they'd actually run it

But, she said.

What?

Maison Bado.

I know, I'm sorry. You'd think they'd have gotten the name of the house right

She looked at him. Not just the house. Not even my name.

Anywhere? He took the magazine, turned pages. Hell. I'm sorry. But doesn't mean anything. You know what it's like to put together a journal, all the little pieces you can't find in time to go to press. A stupid mistake.

Bado on the phone then, demanding correction.

Then more weekends. Soon among the joyous company of big men were women, bright dresses and flowers and lipstick and hats birding the entryway, Bado with a sheen on his cheeks.

What? he said.

What? she said.

He always had to have people, bloodshot without them. In the villa men and women slept not just in the guest rooms but on the sofa and in two Bibendums shoved together.

Bado a bit of a reptile, she thought, watching him gleam in others' eyes. Bado frivolous, she thought, as he and his men whooped down the stairs, collapsed with women in the sun box.

Why do you always need so many people? she whispered.

Why do you want so few?

And gradually the idea was growing. Accidental at first, but when people spoke of Villa Bado, did he stop it?

And then there was the international convention for architects held on a ship steaming to Athens. Glamorous modern Mediterranean at once. Invitations went out, one came to Villa Bado, to Bado.

The ship was to sail from Marseille. She could sit in a chair she'd designed, on the deck she'd designed, with her hand holding a drink on a table she'd designed, in a house she'd designed, and watch the ship full of designers steam by.

Bado had been packing, taking care with his clothes, hunting for his special corkscrew.

So she poured a glass of cold wine and drank it hot out on the deck. Went back inside to the bar she'd made so beautiful, the light sifting invisibly from a secret place above, bottles and glasses turned to jewels. Poured another.

Please, he said, behind her. Don't sulk. You wouldn't go if you were invited.

Might.

You know perfectly well you wouldn't. You'd hate it.

Not the point.

I don't know why you weren't invited

Because my name appears nowhere

We've gone over that and over that

The next day she walked with him up the path to the train for Marseille. And when his train had rattled away, she stood for a moment in the quiet, walked back. Stood on her shiplike terrace, staring at the beautiful sea beautiful sky, thinking, Hate. The problem always with people like this. If they want your love they want everyone's love and are never true, never. And now he's filled this place, it's him.

Your fault, she thought. You built it as the expression of him, you thought of it all, how he holds his face when he shaves so needs a mirror that will rise, and how he tears off his jacket when he enters so needs a rack at elbow height, how he moves too excited between coffee and layouts so needs tables that roll and have surfaces to silence the clatter. So you made these things.

(Love, foolish!) This place was always an emanation of him but one *you* made, and now he's made it his own, what did you expect? But no can't live here anymore.

Bon voyage!

You'd never know to look at her pale dreamy eyes how hard she could be.

Yes she could.

Keys, satchel.

In Totor then, whipping past the cape and along the beach of Menton and then why not she turned hard left and went up, away from the coast, grinding up now along the gorge. Looking.

Weedy fields, groves, vineyards. Meadows. Lemon trees. Air.

We'll sort it out later, she wrote Bado. *You stay in the house. Just now I want something new.*

Eventually he returned from Athens, slept it off, called, wept, but soon enough carried on.

STANDING ON THE SCORCHING TERRACE NOW, NOW, IN 1965, NOT three decades earlier, Eileen presses a hand to her eyes, lets herself be in dark for a moment. Then looks out again, and how extraordinary it is that those days years ago are simply before her, around her, as present as this hot air.

BECAUSE THEN, BACK THEN, AGAIN SHE'D GONE TO TOWN HALL, again signed papers, again written a check. But land away from the coast this time: this land she would own, her name on the title even if, ha, her occupation was listed as *none.*

Again the flat in Menton, again sandwiches and beers at night, again the drives each day to the site, the steep road winding up five miles from the shore. Up there: hot waves of air, seared leaves, the horizon a shiver of light. Late afternoon, dust drifting up after she parked, her shadow before her, she walked up the road running alongside the plot, measuring again by pace the three huge cisterns that formed the lot's edge, and she'd build atop those cisterns, let their stone walls be the base of her aerie. Bon voyage, skinny pilotis! Stone. Half the plot was planted, old lemon trees, gnarled vines. Hopeful.

In this house too, she'd have terraces and sliding glass and shades inside and out that could open or close to dissolve the walls; in this house, too, she'd have shelves and tables that fold from walls, a ceiling eye for private light from the sky, a bedroom that's also a workroom and lounge, cabinets and beds built in. This house would be as sleek and mod as the one by the sea but stern, austere, made only for her—and Louise, her room over the gangplank. And with this house you would not see a thing from the road, just try, just try peering through the gate, try craning to see up those concrete steps to her sunlit retreat. Now that Eileen knew all the craftsmen she'd need, knew them and liked them as they did her, craftsmen she'd made expert in concrete and cork and Bakelite and bent wood, building would be almost a snap.

She'd live there summers with Louise, leave Paris in June, return in September. Work. Cultivate grapes and lemons. Get a tortoise. Give any spare money to unwed mothers. And cats.

After some months, Bado began to call, to drive up. Oh why not, she thought. Fifteen years older than he, she could look at him now from a sage distance, let him fall into shape as the foolish old friend. First he'd show up when she was in the midst of building and it was true he could be helpful when things went wrong (supplies late), very good at getting on the phone and shouting. Then, when the house was done, she'd be up on her terrace or just within the sliding doors drawing, and the doorbell would ring, and from the white gangplank she'd see him standing down by his car. He'd take off his hat, smooth his hair, an oil gleam of scalp where it now thinned. Forty-one. Barely thirty when they'd met! But then he'd look up at her on the terrace and lose three years in his smile. Oh Bado. At least now he had what he'd wanted. Le G went to the house by the sea all the time. Weekends and even long weeks, Bado and Le G and strange little Von and the jolly company of men.

And she had what she'd wanted, too. Insulation.

Some isolate others insulate all

What you did was willful, friends said. Just walking away from that house? Not smart.

I had to, she said.

But what will happen to it, I mean, the title?

Oh Bado and I will sort it.

Have you got on paper that you bought the land, that you made it?

Not to worry, she said. I designed it, my drawings, my words, anyone can tell, for heaven's sake he's no designer and his French

Floating about in her house in the hills

Still waiting for the phone to ring

From?

Anyone wanting her to make them a house. Or hotel or community center or city. She was experimenting constantly, up there surrounded by drawings. Modular housing and holiday centers for workers, with nurseries and theaters and workshops and cafeterias. Models scattered around the tiled floor of her new bedroom-study-lounge, models with wide scallops of seating or rippling raylike roofs.

But why would anyone call when no one even knows who I

That's not true.

Still, phone not ringing.

Well can just carry on making things for myself, what's wrong with that.

It's a waste, said friends and then Pruny, Pruny by then was not only born but a teenager. Time!

After you got rid of your shop and everything to build a house, he gets it, your masterpiece? Auntie? Why don't you go out and make people see you, demand they pay attention like others do—like Le G does?

Just not like that.

And it's true that from time to time (silent house, hands drawing and cutting) a feeling would rise in her throat.

What if it stuck, the mistake?

THEN ONE DAY IN HER NEW HOUSE IN THE HILLS: A POSTCARD. ON one side, the Parthenon, a row of white columns against bright blue. On the other, *Chère mademoiselle! How I regret your absence from our festivities at the house by the sea, given how your living spirit speaks forth from the walls!*

In the corner, by his signature, was one of his cartoons: tall broken columns, a puff of cloud, a bow-tied, hatted man. Him. He had slung a foot on a tumbled pediment and turned to look through glasses at the viewer—at Eileen holding the card in her hand.

She saved it. Who wouldn't. Put it in a box of such things she'd burn glamorously one day near the end, on a roof.

Went about her business (not business), pretending she wasn't aware of that house down there below the vineyards and hills and haze, the men in her rooms.

Then, months later, or already a year? another postcard. Three plump naked women heaped on a rug, bottoms and hips and dark-rimmed eyes.

Chère mademoiselle! Again I rue being unable to spend time with you in your house. I would be delighted to relate how these days let me appreciate again its rare spirit and form—so dignified, charming, full of wit. I wish you would join our company as I would like to discuss with you a great many things.

A line was drawn from *your house* to the bottom of the card and, in small print, *We both know you are the genius of this place.*

Sliver of pleasure.

Looked at the words again, almost laughed.

Well.

Good.

She smoothed the card with the side of her hand and placed it with the other in her box. Proof.

And then, the following summer—was it already '37?—Bado called and said, Le G's been here all week, keeps talking about you, the house, he has a model of it on his desk in Paris, that's what he told me, that's how much he admires the place. Anyway he begs me to get you down for a weekend

No

Wants to ask you something

Oh

Maybe *to collaborate*— Please, Bado said, come for lunch.

So, so, so, so. Yes, down she drove.

6

MONDAY

Down by the sea, in the cabin on the earthen terrace, Le G does not yet remember any of this. No, he's shaving, but if he remembered (if his body did) then his hand with the razor and his cheek pulled long for the blade's stroke might recall the morning of that lunch, nearly thirty years ago: 1937?

He'd been shaving then, that summer, while staying in Bado's villa, thinking how delightful, how simple yet clever, that just touching a small mirror made it spring forward, so that you felt you were with something alive, with the spirit, the genius, of the place.

Genius: not a word he used often.

And the genius here was in such intimate correspondence with his own, had indeed arisen from it! *That* genius and his own primary genius here mingled to make this villa. Masculine spirit meeting feminine form.

Homage, flattery, yet piquing.

What were the possibilities?

He was shaving as Von fussed over outfits before lunch, liking costumes lately, had taken to wrapping a scarf around her head, glittery dresses, her mouth a spot of black lipstick, as he stood with hips near the window ledge, shoulders and back bare to the Mediterranean sun. He swirled Bado's nickel brush in the dish of foam, painted it on his skin, and again how pleasing not to lean to the mirror—and there was his face, afroth, in a disk of glass upon the wide blue sea.

Homeric, he felt, as he drew the blade through foam.

Yes he was now a man whose body filled its height, a man of heft and substance. His *prime.* Liked the feel of that word in his mouth. A man who had grown inward and outward and all over the world, steaming on the *Massilia* to Brazil (only now realizing that Massilia was ancient Marseille, lived in by ancient Mediterranean men), then steaming on the *Giulio Cesare* (of course!) to Rio, flying to New York, lecturing at Princeton and Harvard, being written up for his outrageous statements, having designs stolen by Volkswagen and the Russians, but inventing marvels, too, the brise-soleils, the Modulor Man just beginning to stir inside him, plans for cities.

And not just these outward travels but his intimate ones, his necessary personal travels, because things that are needed must be had.

A high point: the era of two queens: black American dancer and white Nordic princess. He'd written both enraptured letters the same week: only one who does that writing knows how keen the pleasure. Josephine in Rio and then on the ship from Rio, beautiful funny Josephine! He'd drawn her dancing, drawn her sweet body as she'd slept, gone to a shipboard costume party with her. Her dancing was like his architecture, yes, they shared the spirit of the modern. A shame she was already taken: too little time. And then Marguerite! with her blond hair and money, driving in her sedan over New Jersey skyways, his fingers pushing through her fur coat and under the band of skirt and silky slip until they slid to smooth skin, the subtle feel of muscle deep in a hip as she shifted a gear then placed generous gloved fingertips on the flex of his trousers.

Or that journalist somewhere, or that student. No need to care that other skin contained other life, so he would sink his teeth into a woman's bottom, bite until she'd squeal and smack and rub the smarting crescent. He'd measure his women not with numbers, women were at odds with numbers, with masculine rationality, only the male form was a true measure, a ruler, so he'd measure his women with hands, teeth, tongue. Place his thumb at hip bone, middle finger at navel, pivot like a compass and the middle finger reached the other hip bone, pivot twice and it reached a nipple. Record her only that way: the sensual.

Meanwhile he'd send Von reports of his private motions: his temperature, bowel movements, diet. Von, his heart, his hearth.

And he'd send his mother a grand version of the public motions. Mother, you should see how they speak of me here!

Yet still. He looked at the eyes in the mirror above the streaks of pink cut through foam. Yet still, all these women, whores and mother and wife, red and blue and yellow rooms, did not yet make a whole. Something more was needed, a synthesis of these primary colors, something supreme—

NOW, IN HIS CABIN, AS LE G SHAVES, HE IS NOT THINKING OF THE past, certainly not of that day almost thirty years ago, that lunch. Bado is gone, as is Von, and his mother, and all the other women who might have flowed through his thoughts that day. He's alone, a rock with the greenery and sand washed away.

No, one woman's left: Madame R, who'll be over in a minute for the morning shot. Then he has got to finish Venice, get it done and gone.

7

MONDAY

Oh yes, that lunch is still clear in E's memory. Forget memory. It is still right here in front of her face as she stands on the terrace, hands on the rail, measuring tape in her pocket, sun battering down, the vast valley before her.

That day, that lunch. Her palms hot on the steering wheel but heart calm, motoring down to the house by the sea for the first time in several hard years. Parking by the station, walking the path along the tracks, descending the narrow steps, turning.

Le Grand waited at her entryway.

Glinting glasses, smiling, her *Enter slowly* over his head.

This moment isn't a piece of time but a painting.

Mademoiselle, he said, and bowed and offered his arm. At last, he said. What a pleasure.

Then he led her inside her house.

The others are looking into the meal, he said, the only time my madame lives is when stirring a pot, although perhaps such a thing is not familiar to you, being a woman unlike any other, and I should say at this juncture (passing through the curving entry, his tall body close) that I've come to see the intelligence, the intentionality, here, how this entry says, Come in please but I shall guard my secrets at first.

And as they walked past surfaces she'd made of polished aluminum or frosted glass or glossed tile he murmured, Yes here too it all became clear, the spirit of the place is sensuality, isn't it, the entrancement through slight sensual revelations and then concealments, so provocative

(Yes E remembers these words, so that now, staring up into the blue, she thinks it is the air around her, this remembering.)

Bado and Von called, Lunch, lunch! and how strange it was to be called by them there, to have one of her own blue glasses handed her by the thin birdlike hand of Von, eyes still like a silent movie star's, and to see Bado, more stringy less gleam in him now, standing shadowed against the light still so brilliant. Then the four sat at a table on the side of the house away from the sun, near the lemon trees.

Santé!

Zum Wohl!

Prost!

Chin-chin, is that what they say in England? No ah mademoiselle is not English forgive me but Irish. Ah, Vonny, just look at what you've made for us! And Bado thank you yes please pour again and how interesting that this glass is blue that it hides what it holds just as the plates are frosted, an interesting opacity in so much here, like the entrance with that curious integument between outside and in—

And so on, as around went Eileen's dishes heaped with urchins, bouillabaisse, mussels, greens, as they ate and listened to the great man, and Bado opened another bottle and another, the light slowly fading, crickets coming to life, Von's eyes growing sunken, mouth dark.

We are a funny group, Le G said in the quiet. The four of us here. No child among us. And plenty of opportunities, I imagine. No, our generativeness is only in the things we make. But I must confess that I feel something in the air here, I have all week since arriving. As if in the air itself of this house is a spirit, almost a child, your child. I positively feel something stirring to life

Mermaid, said Von.

Pardon? said Eileen.

The others waited. Von's eyes dulled, chin fell.

You know, said Le G, how smoke inhaled by walls leaks out later as spots? That is how it is here, I think: the desire you two perhaps had for a child

Pardon?

soon must make itself manifest in the walls, and you shall find your child drawn there. You shall draw your child out of the wall. A birthing by house. A parthenogenesis!

He looked at Eileen, cigarette clenched between his teeth.

Virgin birth, I mean.

I know, she said, what it means.

I should have realized forgive me but let me elaborate

Then at some point the light was gone, the red of the entry was rust, Von was asleep at the table, Bado slumped in his chair. Only E and Le G alert.

She is mostly like this, he said, stroking Von's hair. I have tried for years to stop her. But how? Anyway I've been meaning to speak to you but didn't want to embarrass poor Bado

Of course but why poor

Oh you know what I mean, he is an entertaining man and loving but must be loving because he has so little else to offer, no? As I said you are the genius of this place, yet he, well. But this matter I wanted to discuss and I hope you'll be interested, the temple I'm making in Paris to the spirit of modernity, I'd like, well I'd like you to join with me on it yes? Ah then you might let me show you the current version, let me go down to get it or if you wouldn't mind as the model's a bit cumbersome

So of course she smiled nodded got up to take glasses to the kitchen first, and yes what was in her was hope.

Hope!

Hope and a lot of wine and it was already dark, better be careful. Then there she was stepping down her spiral stairs, and how strange, this spiral she'd first drawn out of sheer air, now a place she trod in the dark, feeling foreign.

Downstairs, dim. Quiet, scarcely the sound of waves, just her feet, her heels, tiny clockings on tile. She felt a sudden absurd moment as if a child, the old panic of stepping into darkness a nervous hand quickly held out, but then she rounded the corner and inside the guest room she could just make him out, dark shape in the dark. But he stepped forward and seemed to be in a fur, yes, fur draped over shoulders, legs bare.

He smiled. Ah you've come. I was just admiring, as you know I admire so much of this house, these spiral steps, a perfect decision. Screwing the house into the stone. For a moment I thought that something less fragmented might have been better, a Pythagorean screwlike ramp, with more continuum, but

No the angle was too sharp

Yes precisely so you'd need steps, and then to articulate the spiral again but in plan at the roof in that lovely glass nautilus, well it's so very pleasing and makes me think again of how intimately this house weds the sensual with the rational and emotional, the surfaces at once so alluring yet suggesting

Well we did mean for surfaces to capture the senses and thereby be a portal to

Please no need to say *we.*

Ah. She leaned against the wall, her wall, yet somehow not

You and I know, he went on, his voice low in the stairwell, that you designed alone, at once making both this house and its maker sublimely singular. And this is what I most wanted to say to you, mademoiselle, or discuss with you rather, that you have struck me profoundly as a singular synthesis of so much, it's uncanny. Not only a synthesis of the rational sensual and emotional, but also in a more rare manner both the ancient, forgive me, you smile but I think you know what I mean, the ancient and the most fabulously modern, and I've already mentioned my temple to the modern spirit in Paris to showcase the most original specimens of modernity in our age and your work must be in it. Bado, little as he understands these things, has told me much of your design for a new holiday center and shown me drawings that make clear it's yet another piece of innovation bespeaking the best principles of our age my principles foremost ha yes I do flatter myself so please you must exhibit this project in my temple. Yes, good. I'm glad especially because you yourself are, as I was saying, please don't blush mademoiselle, almost a temple in yourself. I know I go too far, but I am forthright, you have become to my innermost symbologizing mind a temple both exquisitely modern and ancient, indeed what I think is that you are, and this embarrasses even me to say but I am courageous, you are a veritable Parthenon, don't laugh, I shall go and blurt out all I've been holding in my heart, the way in which you conflate the sensual the rational the emotional, I am a synaesthete you know, and I understand that you have a touch of this trait too? seeing sounds in color and hearing fragrances? I see these qualities of the sensual rational and emotional as colors red and blue and yellow and it's so rare to find all in one especially a woman and if you mixed these primary colors as light you'd get white as you know the ultimate purity the ideal again a Parthenon, white and fine and clean-boned especially now rid of the gaudy misbegotten color fusing these elements and I neglected to say that a further way in which you synthesize is in the sexes or sexualities perhaps better term what with your earlier liaison with that chanteuse I know I go too far please wait don't go ah no please bear with me you've heard my argument thus far it's so rare that I would bare myself to anyone like this only you yes you synthesize not only the trinity of human qualities and thus the trinity of primary colors into purest form but also the diverse sexualities and in doing so you become most complete, most perfect, you are that temple of ancient perfection and modern spirit at once. And that you built this wonder of a house in response to me my principles yet so empathetically so passionately it can only make me feel as though I have been honored and in turn I wish to honor you and what can I say but that when one approaches a temple one wishes to honor, one makes an offering and this is what I meant most to say, most to ask, mademoiselle, accept what I bring!

And he dropped the fur robe.

Quiet now. Just the light on his glasses, his bare shoulders and belly and scraggle of hair. Heavy sound of breathing; a wave washing through pebbles.

But perhaps, he said after a long moment, judging by your silence and those eyes quite unreadable, perhaps I have been mistaken. I see. Although the signs were I thought quite clear. A mouth and entering, as you put it. Sensuality, as you said. How it atrophies in machinelike design. You were, I think, quite clear.

But I see now this is all the same modus. Or perhaps what I've so mistakenly admired instead conceals frigidity.

Yes, he said, and he stepped now into full light, pulled up a naked handful of himself, rubbed.

Does this look like atrophy to you, he asked. Do you see any atrophy here?

ENOUGH. EILEEN RUNS A HAND OVER HER HOT FACE.

Inside. Glass of water.

AUNT? PRUNY SAYS ON THE PHONE THAT NIGHT. I CAN TELL BY YOUR voice. Shall I come? You know from St. T it's only a few hours.

No, no.

But don't you think we could or you could

No. There's nothing to be done. One thing led to another, we've gone over the chain a thousand times. Nothing to be done.

EXCEPT, SHE THINKS AFTER SHE'S HUNG UP, LYING IN BED IN THE dark, except go down there and burn.

The terraces along the coast, where Eileen built her white villa and Le Grand built his cabin beside it: these terraces are three thousand years old, built by Ligurians, long before the Romans. Built one by one to keep this Alpine land from sliding into sea, to turn rough shrubland and woods into vineyards and groves. It's hard work. Stand on steep, rocky ground, hack with a pick, then shovel deep, pry up a rock from the slanting earth, lean hard with your foot to pry it free, roll it over to the pile. Then hack and shovel and pry again, gradually cut into the earth a squared edge, and set the stones against it. Again. Slowly turn slanting mountainside into rows of earthen steps, then plant. A white wine's been made here for two thousand years, and there are olive trees as old. They're still here, their growth tortured but shapely, a knot.

8

MONDAY NIGHT

All day Le Grand has been irritated by that writer's questions. He's paced from cabin to workshop, up the steps, along the path to the tip of the cape and back, staring through eucalypts and pines at the glittering sea, bobbing yachts, doing anything but climbing down to the rocks to swim, although that's all he wants to do (heart), he wants only to have water envelop him. Why his aesthetic transformation from the pure and smooth, his early villas so delicate and poured in fine white concrete, to the later work, apartment buildings or whole cities made of rough stone or crude concrete, work that felt wrenched raw from the earth? Forces at work. Currents. A man like himself (artist, swimmer, diver) naturally follows not only currents flowing around him but (more essential) (more potent) currents within, from those wellsprings of soul, of genius. To explore those currents now consciously is his duty to himself as artist.

Now he's at his usual station after dinner, on the whiskey crate dragged back into the shack, dirty armskin gleaming in the overhead bulb, feet bare and dirty on bare dirty floor, goat toenails of one foot scratching other one pleasantly, as his damp wrists (must blot) hover above the paper while he inks in a Modulor Man. Another tiny Modulor Man. Could have someone in the office do this of course but it's soothing, banal, frees the mind to roam.

Heavy paws pacing.

Had forgotten about that.

To have dreamt he was pregnant! He! With a cat.

Curious how dreams flash up.

But that is not relevant now. No. What's on his mind is that shift, the inquisitor's question, that's the mystery he'll try to penetrate as he inks in another tiny man, each lying in a bed in the Venice cemetery-hospital, looking up.

Von's little bone in his pocket, there. He holds it tenderly as he gets up, pushes open the door, steps out to the darkness, sparkle of stars and lights in the cove, fresh mineral smell, sound of waves washing through pebbles.

The shift within his aesthetic.

Not the War, as that fellow says, but something like it.

Violence.

Yes.

Violence. Something done to him?

Maybe. Maybe yes.

Something that ripped open the surface that had gone soft, just as his hands had ripped open that ancient fusty European idea of home, with its lace and carved décor, and instead gone straight to bone, his white buildings machines stripped of ornament. And then, a decade later, yes, the end of the thirties, there would be another rip, his hands plunging through surface again to reach the real.

Yes, he thinks. It was likewise a rip of my skin that led me to that fresh raw aesthetic! It was the *propeller* that propelled me.

Around his thigh, the spiral of stitches. His naked leg testimony to what was done to him and how he endured.

Remember this carefully.

HE'D COME DOWN TO THE HOUSE, BADO'S VILLA, HE'D NEEDED A rest, he'd had an awful year, a year of blows. Keys, Bado, he'd said in Paris, I need a few weeks, maybe a month, you're not going down, are you? Let me have the place.

And down from Paris in his green Fiat he drove with Von to swim and eat fish and drink cold wine and draw, recover in salt water salt air. By then yes he was someone who could make a fellow like Bado hand over his keys, a man who'd grown in every direction, inward and outward and all over the world. The years of two queens! American dancer and Nordic princess! While Von always waited at home tap-tapping her shoe and feeding her birds, and his mother waited at the mailbox for his letters.

Yet still, in his prime, he received blow after blow, and as he thinks about this closely, looking over the bay to the next cape, beyond which is another bay and another cape, and on it goes around the sea, *his* sea, now he recognizes that the blow of the propeller was only the articulating blow, knocking him from one phase of mind to the next.

While he and Von stayed in the villa that summer he'd swum daily, of course (tonic, his regimen), and so was swimming the cove, stroking through green water that fell away cool and delicious at his legs, gazing with each splashing turn of the head up at the shaggy cliff, moving with a strong and regular rhythm, when suddenly he was struck with terrific force from behind and plunged into an undersea cavern. He looked up shocked underwater, in roiling foaming froth, a white boat flying over him, until he bobbed up to air and saw his thigh transformed, a sheet of skin sliced loose by the blade yet still attached along one seam to his leg, floating like a mottled ray in a sea of pink foam, and at that he beat the water with his fists.

You've run me over!

But as he floated in the bloody froth, shock transformed pain and began to work something inside him (he sees now), as if he'd needed this violence to recognize his contempt, his hatred, for the white and smooth and pure: sterility: he despised it. He lusted now for splatter, shag, the rough and animal and wild, for color and crudeness and bristle.

He was hoisted from the water and carried to a hospital, where he refused anesthesia, only more of the tremendously exciting pain as two meters of suture were stitched by a steel needle through his skin to yoke the floating ray back to boned leg. Who knew pain could be so inspiring? Could produce the images he saw as he gripped the metal table and howled, his mouth like the center of the propeller, howling curses at the bloodied doctor and nurses struggling to hold him?

But yes, that blow was only the final clarifying stroke after a year of outrages from which he had come to the sea house to mend. The first insult had come from the house, after all, from that woman or whatever she was. He had invited her to join him! Proposed a collaboration! Yet been rebuffed! Whereas Marguerite with her furs and golden hair and money adored him, played with him in the Carlton, took him to her beach bungalow! And whereas Josephine had dallied with him in Rio and then on the ship! Whereas sweet Von adored him. Whereas women like this. Versus that half woman.

And then there'd been the debacle of his modern temple in Paris: no one came, no one reviewed it, even that woman sent a *servant* in her place.

Then the debacle of his first solo show of paintings, which he (secret) cared about most, rising each morning at six to paint. No one came—ten rooms of paintings! Plaintive cries of brilliant canvases in the dark. Another slap to his soul.

So as is now clear the physical manifestation of these attacks was the propeller. Smooth white sharp, as if it were the white villa itself, as if it were that woman, as if it were all the world more smooth and full of grace than he, ever the bleeding octopus pounded upon rocks.

So then: of course: punishment. For as his blood flowed into the cove's water, an idea began stirring within. Although he didn't know it until after the stitches, the mending, when he was back in the villa, in the bed down in the guest room, when he woke with an urge.

In salty sheets on his back he'd fingered his little spoonful in its tangle of hair until that purplish pulp had swelled and tautened, become the eggplant muscle rising as ever, waving as he lay back and pondered it.

Didn't want that just then, though.

Yet something, some other craving, grew, until he was up. Feet dirty on her clean tiles.

Something to do with this place. These walls.

Dirty them. Furious desire to dirty them.

Up the spiraling staircase, the screw into the rocks, as if that wouldn't lead a man's thoughts, up around that coy red bend, likewise meant to tease and leave a man swollen, to the kitchen, where Von's hand trailed smoke, steam blooming her solemn thin face. A kitchen so mean, so small. For of course that woman had never cooked a meal. Far from Von, far from a generous and *real* woman.

What moved him through the house, staring through hard disks of glass at each subtle gleaming surface she had devised to trick and amaze, what moved him was the opposite of desire. It was *against*: against that woman, against fineness, purity, whiteness: against her walls.

Standing naked, legs apart: be the rude boy spattering.

In the living room, then, in the parlor or salon or whatever she called it, the main room, which faced the sea, he went with a stick of charcoal as a man would have used twenty thousand years ago, a man like himself, of torn skin and muscle and blood and oily palms and sweat and stink, downright stink, a natural man doing what a man most naturally does to leave a mark on his world.

He walked over the tiles to the wall lit by his own glorious Mediterranean sun and reached up, he was tall, he reached high up the white wall, the fine white wall she had placed just there to counter the one beside it and screen the living area from another secret bedroom, with her it was all screens and veils and mirages, he stood before this contrived wall and crushed his stick of charcoal against it and drew a long black smudging line that went down then curved and became a huge breast then a punched-in waist and then up for another ballooning breast, two of them to clutch or press your tongue into, bite, and then his hand swung down from there and drew a great round hip and buttock, really a rump is what it was, rump like a horse's, enormous fat rump that was round enough to grab and heave where you wanted, and then he curved in again to squiggle little insignificant legs because why should he care about them, locomotion, he didn't care, why let her go anywhere, and back up to her other great round hip, and he was hard drawing this, drawing this woman, a real woman, on the wall before him, forcing her to be there on the smooth frigid wall that that woman had built to amaze and insult him. Right beside her *Invitation au voyage*, another of her cold enticings, which was nothing, just abstract, nothing at all, whereas what he did was real, was an *act*, and in doing so he said *fuck* to her whiteness and smoothness, he said *fuck* and *fuck* to her, and yes what he made was a form, not just lines but form that needed color, and the paint pots were on the table in the precious bedroom-workroom-lounge or whatever she called it, rows of paint pots for coloring god knows whatever precious projects she once did, and Bado left them there to give the illusion that he did anything, that he created anything, which of course he hadn't and couldn't, only Le G did, and now his hot feet slapped over her tiles and he had the little pink paint pot open as well and a cool creamy blue and god it felt good, the creamy paint, it felt sublime against his most tender yet firm slim muscle, and what a fine wand this was to paint with, to slide along the sleek wall slick, and here, if he leaned, no, pushed, into the wall, here he could leave a clear imprint, tangle of hair, because what he was doing was creating the real, the animal, and not just a wet swirl of hair from there but a large print of belly, swollen angry and pressed hard against her wall in pale pink, and you could even make out the navel, tender little knot, and below it the jumble of hair and then a streak of muscle and bursting vein—

Smoke.

Von stood small and dark at the window.

He breathed hard, hands shaking. From his thumb fell a long drip of pink.

Von drew slowly on her cigarette, smoke drifting over the glassed blue sky. She stepped over to look, and her looking made him look, as if his own hands had not just put the thing there. A rumpy woman, pink and black, striding, breasts as wide as hips, walking into a red-edged whelk. Smoke leaked gently from Von's face.

He pressed his palm against the wall beside his naked woman and left a wrinkled print, as an ancient man in a cave would do. Because he *was* an ancient man, and did what a man must do.

Her, she said.

He nodded.

That was the first. An infection hot in his blood as he moved through the villa on the edge of dream, Von appearing now and then as through mercury, black eyes, shadows on the floor and walls. He waved them away, stalked on, composing. Points in an argument, in a plan: a trapeze in which his mind hung as he paced up and down the spiral stairs and out to the terrace and back into this house, which in truth had been his all along. He'd guided the hand here, been the figure to whom the maker of this house made an offering. She or he or properly *it* had been an amanuensis, executing his vision. This house was his.

Yes: and he'd been flowing (currents inside him) toward just this for a time, needing only that propeller to jet him forward.

In New York, tipping his hat to a dreadful lady who'd dragged him up to her apartment, too spare, bony, nothing alive, he did not want to fuck her after all, could not collaborate with her cold spare flat. Madame, your walls do not speak to me.

A wall must do more than perform its simplest function. Painting upon it in one act I demolish it and create an ineffable space.

One must stand within walls and light them with painting. Horses, fish, generous women. Eyes are projectors, beams of vision cast out to enliven walls around you. Some might call this solipsism. But properly understood it is true absorption in what lies beyond you: self-dissolution pure.

This house would become his museum.

He would compose a promenade of paintings. At the entrance that so irritated him—that curving red shell that made a man twist and turn as already he saw the room he longed to enter—just at that entrance he'd make a painting that swallowed her *Enter slowly.* Large figure, yellow and red. Enter slowly? No: he'd smash in as he liked. A tiny slit in her triangle, running his finger up and down the wet paint of the slit and making hard holes of the nipples.

Mademoiselle: I enter however and whomever I like.

Around the teasing red curve would be the rumpy woman in the salon, who coaxes one into her shell, into the sea, luring him as this woman had done, luring him to humiliation and outrage. Siren! Dentata! The propeller itself! Next in the dining room an abstracted version of his own self being ripped open by the blade of the yacht, a red mouth forever howling, blood-red upon the inky sea.

And the masterpiece. By the black sandbox, a portrait of the monsters who thought they'd conceived this house themselves, the eunuch and the half woman.

He drew with a knife, cutting into the wall. To the right he drew Bado, soft and hulking with a tiny thumb of a penis and punching bags of manly breasts. To the left, that woman, monumental but legs akimbo and arm flung back in ecstasy, a pair of nipples like thimbles jutting into the sky. Between these two misbegottens: the baby they (were they not unnatural) might have conceived.

Plaster dust silted the wrinkled side of his hand, clung to the fur of his arm and the fur crawling downward. He would use a burnt stick to incise each line, blacken it, that most marvelous primitive instrument. He was the most ancient man, here with a pool of Mediterranean sun burning his bare foot.

I am just pulling it out of the walls, he would say. As the cave painter pulled from rock walls creatures that lived secretly within: bison, horses. I pull what has been latent all along, the secret form of life trapped within. I am delivering for you your baby.

ON THE LAST DAY OF THIS PASSIONATE SUMMER, HE WAS STANDING, naked—as he liked to wipe his hands on bare legs and be even more unified with the project, holding a charcoal stick to wall, other hand hovering almost forgotten near his haunch—when Von called him.

He turned: camera click.

His large manly rump faces the camera, while his more potent manly muscle faces the work, suture scar twining about his thigh. He looks at the camera with an eye of affronted innocence.

An image in which he will delight.

Of her, to her, for her.

At her.

My dear mademoiselle, he will say, *see how rich our collaboration is. Look at these glorious graffiti! And I offer them free of charge.*

NOW LE G RESTS A HAND UPON HIS STOMACH AND LOOKS OUT TO sea in the dark. He shifts his gaze from the sparkling shoreline to the slabs of rock at the edge of the cove, then just below: the villa. Its tattered banner hangs limp in the night, its walls gleaming bone. He reaches down and takes himself in forefinger and thumb, streams out a hissing arc.

9

TUESDAY

So how goes it this morning, Pruny asks.

Thoughts do stitch themselves across the brain at night.

Pruny is silent, and then: I know you say it yet I just don't see that there's absolutely nothing

No.

But

Pruny, there is no point.

But couldn't you just

Do you know, E says, there's an old couple across the road who go walking every day but not quite together. They're small. She marches ahead and he comes along slowly with a stick, they both wear hats, and she walks back and forth back and forth quickly while she waits for him to catch up. Tells everything about their . . .

What?

Marriage.

Pruny is quiet a moment. I think you're making a point but am not sure what.

E sighs. So how goes it with you, dear? How is *David*?

A short laugh from Pruny. That's a little mean, Auntie. His hat was still hanging in my studio when I left, so there's that. He's on holiday. With the family.

Just keep painting. All you have total say in.

I can be there in three hours, and we can go together

Pruny, I can't undo anything.

You can make him apologize.

And then what? A man like him does not feel remorse.

Make him feel awfully sorry then.

Haunt him? Shall I haunt him? Burn down his cabin?

Yes!

Thank you for calling, dear. Bye now.

ALWAYS DISCONCERTING THE MOMENT AFTER HANGING UP, HAVING to place yourself back where you are.

Now feeling nettled.

Everything Pruny wants her to do should have been done years ago, she did what she could, wasn't enough, there we are.

Haunt him.

Anyway: the goals for today. Prepare three rough sketches for the extension itself and then consider the garden, how the plantings can be reoriented. And have a look at the S-chairs Graham's got, remeasure them to make sure you indeed have the numbers correct in your cahier and it's the gallery that's wrong, as this should be corrected. In fact let's start with the chairs (lazy) while sipping tea.

From her satchel she pulls out the cahier, finds the pages for the S-chair, there we are, and smooths them with the back of her hand. Let's have a look, compare my original drawing in the cahier with a live model of one of the first versions out there on the terrace, isn't it handsome still, and here's your tape measure, good, glad it's still shady enough to see numbers where's my loupe

You are taking your cahiers? Louise had asked as Eileen packed.

Well to double-check the chairs, E said. But she saw Louise's mouth set, and Pruny with one boot kicking silently at the air, and she knew that Louise thought this record-keeping was an absurd way to spend time and Pruny thought if she was going to have anything corrected, settle any accounts, then obviously she should— But E just said, You know how dispiriting it is to have one's work misrepresented. Furthermore if the gallery's saying that someone wants to buy the rights to make them then the numbers must be correct.

And you know, she added, I did once tear off the labels at an exhibit where they said everything was someone else's, when it was mine. So.

Fabulous, Auntie! Forceful.

All right. Anyway. Might be an obsession and a small one at that but still she's determined to take her loupe and examine each photograph and journal review of her work that she'd pasted in her cahiers and rid each review of errors, typing a note, pasting it to the page. Louise calls the cahiers scrapbooks, annoying, as they're more than that, professional records of all E's made, all that she shall leave behind, because god knows no one else has paid enough attention. Some people publish a so-called *oeuvre complète* every few years spewing everything out like an oyster its million eggs, well she's not such a narcissist wouldn't send her accounts into the world, no they're just for her. She's outlived anyone who cares (almost) and anyone who knows (almost) but cannot bear the record that sails out after she's shuffled off her mortal et cetera to be wrong.

Well then why doesn't she do what Pruny wants?

Because there's nothing to be done! A clear chain of events. Her mistake. Bado's haplessness. The monster's outrage. The auction. Done.

Wrinkled trembling finger looms enormous beneath the loupe on the page.

Look, already a fresh correction is needed in one of the reviews.

The chair was never covered in this frail shade of blue! It was always a deep slate.

She swivels to the typewriter and bangs out a note, she likes her black-and-chrome typewriter (*a house should be as practical as a typewriter* no don't think this not his words again), admires the satisfying directness of see and punch and see. *The chair ~~wsa~~ was never covered in this frail shade of blue! Always a deep slate.*

She scrolls out the sheet, places it on her layout board, with trembling X-Acto blade slices it free, glues it into her cahier.

Objectionable comments in otherwise positive reviews she has blocked out with black marker, firm wet stroke and gone. Sometimes blacking out isn't enough, though, and she's taken her blade and cut out a whole passage from an article and thrown it away. There.

Furniture designed with the help of a girlfriend, for instance.

No. We are looking at your work. Not what some monster said about it

Monster! Monster! she can hear Beauty calling in Cocteau's film, the fur slinking off the bed by magic

No, the base of that lamp was originally an ostrich egg

fur slinking off his bare shoulders

Back to the typewriter, bang

What we can be proud of his having a house as practical as a typewriter

No

The musicality of the typewriter yes but the sheer practical machinery of it no. Sensuality instead of

ah sensuality you aim to entrance

IT TOOK SOME WEEKS TO LEARN WHAT HAD HAPPENED AS BADO couldn't bring himself to tell. But then the phone rang, how many years ago, just before the war, and she'd first thought what she always thought when the phone rang heart catching in throat that someone was calling to say, *We've seen your stunning house by the sea and the one in the hills and would love if you'd make one for us could we convince you?* Why yes. But it was never that, never, it was Bado.

When she picked up, the line was silent a moment, but then she heard the waves, and Bado cleared his throat.

Yes? she said. Bado?

Well, he said, and cleared his throat again. Not sure how to tell you this, he said. Something's happened, he said. He's done something. Le G's done something at your house, but I think you'll come to agree when you've had time to reflect that it's really quite wonderful and bold, and I know he meant it as a compliment, as flattery, and it could serve us serve you in the long run.

But she was shaking her head saying, What are you talking about?

He took a breath and tried again. Well it's just that he's done some painting at your house, murals on a few walls, six, maybe eight . . .

And she kept saying, What? Looking at the phone saying, What?

But Bado kept going on about the honor the compliment the

form of *collaboration*, and E remembers Louise standing solid against the glare with a plate of salad, and in the planes of her face E almost saw in shadow and sickly color what Bado was saying over the phone.

When I drove down the other day, Bado said, because you know I'd told him he could have the place a few weeks, when I drove down and saw what he was doing, I tried to stop him of course but I think you know how he can be, absolutely oblivious of anyone

(A squirrel kept climbing through the window one spring. It would knock apples onto the floor, leave smears on the windowsill, its earthy little hands.)

I don't understand.

I'm trying to be clear. Le G has done some paintings on your walls. I think it's a way of

But you don't do such a thing

Well he's not like others as we know

Throw him out, she said. Cover what he's done, two coats of primer, then we'll repaint, I've got primer here, come up and get it

But

What?

I can't

What?

I just can't

Why?

It's his *work*

What?

His work, his painting, you can't just demolish an artist's

The sky was greenish. But she had always seen more green than others, something funny about her eyes, a sex-linked trait, she'd read. She sat with the curve of her S-chair at the curve of her back, its wooden arm beneath her own, receiver in one hand, and looked over the white of her gangway out to the haze of ocean meeting sky.

At some point she hung up.

But she remembers still the glaze over her, over the afternoon, over everything around her, as she moved about the terrace, down to the garden, back up, through the sliding doors, a glaze before her eyes, which were seeing instead those other walls down there and what he had done to them, or what he might have done, because all she could do was imagine and oh imagination is strong.

THEN THE SICKLY PHASE OF NEEDING ACTUALLY TO SEE WHAT HE'D done overtook her, so one day she climbed into Totor and drove down in the sun, the hot road sliding behind her, flying around the deep gorge, fumes in the windows, gassy yellow, too bright, too hot, too fast, and she stopped, wiped her face, looked at her hands shaking on the wheel, turned, and drove home, back to Time.

She'd stay up in her house, be silent. Aloofness was underrated. At least the look of it she could pull off, always had with those pale distant eyes, and pull it off she did, even Louise was impressed, but inside:

Spite or such injury or just wild anger?

Oh but (tilting her face to the sky now up on her terrace, which keeps blurring becoming again the terrace she made three decades ago) just when he did the hideous paintings nothing so minor could possibly matter. In this war she couldn't do anything as she had the last one, too old to drive ambulances. Hard to look any of that in the face in memory and it's not as though she had anything so awful to look at personally. Just blurs of those years, she an Irish lady an enemy to Vichy, resident alien! had to move from even this near the coast, so she and Louise jammed what they could into Totor, drove west, that chill cottage, buckets for stream water, snow, candles, eating potatoes and dandelion greens, rusty chestnuts they'd batter down with brooms. Milk from a friend with a goat, keeping two chickens with blinking eyes, that rabbit they meant to eat but couldn't kill, so had to find greens for it, too. Those wretched years, and wretchedly she did need help from Bado, he as a citizen was free to come and go and was so rueful (again) he made the long drive every month to bring flour and coffee and news. And all along Le G actually scuttled up to Vichy to see what jobs he might get! Collaborator!

Four years after leaving, Eileen and Louise finally drove back through silent yellow fields to her house on the hill. A wreck. German soldiers, followed by looters, had chopped lemon trees, gutted rooms, left drawings and plans and chairs piles of ash, ridiculous pajamas in a puddle of pee. She and Louise stood there, thin ankles in old leather shoes on a floor mostly mud.

Then trying to rebuild, scraping up funds by selling the very last of her rugs and lamps from the shop, ones she'd kept stored, over sixty and starting again, weary, but buck up, she'd said, imagine the hell of others.

And the house by the sea? she asked Bado when he came to see how she was, Bado who'd been able to stay there almost the whole four years but for a month or two, when soldiers took it.

Pretty intact, he said. Still its beautiful self. Though the soldiers did some shooting, a few holes

Where?

Oh (laughing) one of his murals.

Then, more and more as she struggled to replace or mend the broken furniture and walls and tiles at Time, she thought, This has gone on enough, let's sell up here and return to the house by the sea. Sell what I can so there's enough, it's time to shore things up. Bado and I can work something out, lots of room and still quite fond of him in an elder sister sort of way, so possibly pleasant even not to be alone.

But that man was always there.

And worse. She'd managed for what, seven or eight hard years now? to keep her mind clear of precisely what he'd done, but then photos began to appear in his books, those *oeuvres complètes*, those scrapbooks he spewed out to the world once a decade or so, books yes she did buy because she took a professional interest, books in burlap with his name stenciled on as if his work were tea or sugar a staple like that something important heaved aboard ship in a sack, and inside his *oeuvre complète* of '46 were photos of himself in a bomber jacket shot heroic against a stark sky his face sculpted as if a hero, this collaborator! And pictures of his new postwar style, coarse stones jammed into concrete, no more smooth white surfaces now, rough and raw slabs crude but organic, ha.

And the worst. A chapter about his painting. Photo of him astride paint pots and brushes—and suddenly she turned a page and there was her house. Her beautiful transatlantic chair and round glass table with slim chrome throat and beyond them the wide band of sea. Such a shock to see it on a page like that right at her finger

The caption?

Villa Bado

Furniture designed with the help of a girlfriend

Calmly she cut out the page from his book and pasted it in her cahier. Who wouldn't. But those captions she blacked out then cut out then burned, ashes running down the drain, as she grunted with rage.

Which of course made her remember the words all the better.

Furniture designed with the help of a girlfriend

Villa Bado

And the paintings themselves.

Her *Enter slowly* and *No laughing* now had black hairs sprouting below and enormous breasts with hollow nipples, all swelling beneath her wavering loupe as she stared: a vagina and pinching fingers and bottoms and slits and on the next page a man and woman in black and white, he must have cut them right into the wall, the woman with legs bent and arm thrown up nipples pointing upward and the man with a tiny penis like a thumb and between them a floating baby?

Murals at a sea house. Bursting from its dull, sad walls.

That man painting nipply women on her walls down there and those men in her house up here burning her drawings snapping off chair legs throwing them into the fire and going through her drawers pulling out her old pajamas! tossing them on the floor and tromping them with muddy boots

The walls chosen to receive nine large paintings were insignificant. The owner and I witnessed a spiritual transformation throughout as the paintings emerged under the brush. When one opens one's doors to an artist, one gives him speech. When he speaks, one listens

The owner and I

Anger, she typed that night, glass of brandy shaking on the table, *is perhaps the greatest inspiration in those days when the individual is separated in so many personalities. Suddenly one is all in one piece.*

The next morning she called Bado.

Owner.

What?

You witnessed the spiritual transformation.

What?

Stop it. I've seen what he's written.

Ah, he said. All right, he said. Listen

You didn't try to stop him, you encouraged him

He'd already started and you know how he is he doesn't even see, he stalks around and there's nothing

You have never been able to say no to him to stand up you're

That's enough

you're weak and

Enough. Honestly I thought he was right

What?

There's a certain, you have to admit he was introducing something needed, he was complementing the house

What?

Giving it something it needed, a counterpoint to

You sound just like him

It was a form of collaboration

How can you say that

Well when there's a conflation of two

I know what the word means

a conflation of two visions

My vision was not there

But mine *was.*

She laughed, a harsh noise from her throat.

Then silence. Hawk soaring through the valley, wings still.

Oh, Bado said, I can't remember, one of those nights I might have had too much to drink and said something about murals, yes, I might have been drunk and said, Explode the walls!

She could hear in his voice the shiver of joy at his holy union with the great man, his belief that he said, Explode the walls! and Le G took up his words, even though anyone who'd paid attention knew that Le G had said those words first and silly Bado was a parrot.

Then dismay worked into her body, darkness filling her eye, her left eye, that's when this trouble began, her body always absorbed and expressed injuries to her soul and she could not be rid of this darkness, like smoke always before her eye, and then, too, the shake began in her hands, harder to do simple things, Time still such a wreck, half the furniture broken and walls moldered by rain. She could not carry on, had to sell this place in the vineyards, all she wanted was to return to the house by the sea and live there looking at the water having a swim now and then and drinks on the terrace and just make sure she had something to leave Louise and Pruny: all of this stitched through her brain at night.

Finally she called Bado. It's time, she said. I want to come back. We can share, though we must get rid of those murals.

And Bado said with a low wary voice, Yes of course we can share, but about the murals and him, well it's awkward, he does like to come and (voice lower) he's here now.

(For god's sake.)

Restoring the paintings.

(Oh for god's sake.)

He sees this house I think as a sort of museum

A museum!

But then, not long after this, Bado, sad Bado, showed up rumpled on the hot steep road, hat covering the thinning spots, smoky hands limp at his sides. When he was up on her terrace and collapsed in a chair with a Pernod he smiled weakly and asked if he could stay a few days. To which of course a snort of wicked laughter from her but then remorse: he looked so heartbroken. And he let out through his teeth that Le G was at the house working on a project and had invited a cavalcade of architects, and there was no room for Bado.

She petted his hand. They gazed at the yuccas.

Truth is, Bado whispered, I don't know how to get rid of him.

She pondered his face, the new slump of him, so altered. Then went inside for paper.

You do the writing, she said. A handwritten letter seems best.

What a narrow prison you have made for me with your vanity. A correction from you seems necessary. If not, I will do it myself to restore the original spirit of the house by the sea.

10

TUESDAY

Down the winding road to town, along the beach, and out to the cape, past the grove of ancient olives, terraces of lemons, slabs of rock and arcing waves that keep carving coves in the coast, to the dark wooden cabin with a palm frond on the door: Le Grand snores deep and slow. The windows at the cabin's corners are open tonight, and across the dim room drifts a breeze.

Then through mud and water he lurches awake, clutching—at what?—and smacks his hand on the wall. Hand stinging, the room around him again takes form, the form he granted this cube of air fifteen years ago. Faintly lit now with dawn, and through a small window, morning calm.

Where are my bones? she asked. That woman?

That was the question?

He sits on the edge of the bed, hands at knees, and stares into the dimness.

His own bones?

Buried inside this old skin, that's where.

When he stands his body aches as if riddled. Three heavy steps from the bed and he shoves aside the red drape; pressing a hand against the wall, he settles onto the toilet. Rests elbows on thighs, grunts.

His ventilation system: one small window here in this corner facing the slot between cabin and rock, another in the other corner, pulling a current through the place, so that the gases that croak from his rump will blow out over the pines.

Here on the floor by his foot: *The Odyssey. Don Quixote* on his worktable. These books now mean the most to him—the agonies of men! striving and striving but never given what they need! *Quixote* is bound in a little strip of fur of his sweet old Pinceau, his own little Sancho.

Whose jawbone is mounted with a spring.

Where are my bones?

He digs elbows into thighs to focus energies downward and thinks of how, when he'd travel to New York or Chandigarh, he'd write Von every day with news of his bowel movements and temperature. A wife ought to know such things. Why else the drape here instead of a door? Important. In Paris, too, in their flat, the toilet was just a breath from the bed, only a drape between them: Von so ashamed. But he delighted in making her live with proximity, not letting her indulge in the imagined separation of functions in body or place.

A wife *ought* to know such things.

Even if she'd never know what the rest of his body was up to.

With Marguerite and Hedwig and Mitzi and so on.

From the start.

Yes, from the start, or at least once he'd married Von, after the years they'd spent (hidden) in his first little flat, after he'd moved them into the lofty apartment he made. In just one week a letter to Von about his bowel movements; a note to Marguerite, *You can do it, Marguerite, arrange it, I'll be in New York only two days so come to my hotel at ten o'clock, I'll have champagne*; a card to Josephine with a drawing of her and him in Brazil, ah those few happy days he spent with her. All these cards in one week and only he knew, lines in a web all stretching from him, and how pleasurable to pluck a string and know the women trembled from afar.

Why are you thinking this now, old man?

A plume of pain waves through him—and with it the dream: a woman in the dark pulling a bone between her legs.

The wave passes, but not the image. His legs are slick with sweat.

Her spine pulled from between her legs?

Von's bones, all right. The question was about *her* bones.

Well, he could tell you right now where they were and exactly what happened to them. Drinking: drinking until she was so benumbed she couldn't feel her bones dissolve, didn't care when she'd fall. She'd lie laughing, black-tongued, crumpled on the yellow planks, hands waving in the air as if to say, Look at this, look at this terrible comedy, this body I cannot shake.

Wouldn't he lift her carefully, so small, and sit her up, bib her, weep with the effort to make her chew the calcium and red meat, build her up again? Like a child, needing to be made.

Hadn't he spent the last ten years of her life trying to restore her? He can't be to blame.

He has no patience for dreams.

No patience for impotence at the toilet, either.

It's after seven already, he has not even done his calisthenics,

Madame Rebu will knock at the door with her needle any minute, and her boy will be here at noon for Venice. And this ache in his gut, like a rock sewed inside him—

AFTER HE AND TINO HAVE GONE OVER THE VENICE PROJECT, HE SITS back, head hot and damp, and lets the boy roll up the drawings. Then the two go to the fish place for lunch.

Old friend! cries Le G to the boy's father with a heartiness like a gasp, which makes him push himself toward the old man and slap him too hard on the shoulder. Pastis, please!

Tino is at his side, always, his plump anxious face.

But I thought you said, about the pastis

Damn what I said. Don't you agree? We old men should do what we want.

Rebu laughs and pulls down the bottle, and Le G goes out to the terrace. He lowers himself heavy into his chair and squints at the glaring sea, the rocks and cove below.

And there again is Von.

It was from right here that she walked into the water one day, in her dress, scarf around her black hair, nose sharp and pitching her forward. She went down to scold a boy who had pulled a live starfish from the sea and dropped it by his towel on the pebbles. A fleshy starfish. From above, eating lunch, Von had seen this creature drying, dying, in the sun. He could see it, too, if he tried, but who cared?

You won't do anything? she said.

He shrugged, and she turned away but kept looking down, and a line grew between the starfish and Von. Finally she scraped back her chair and limped, furious, down the path to the cove.

He had turned in his seat to watch, sipped his drink, and cartooned the scene. Von who would swallow dozens of sea urchins at a go, their little yellow organs slipping between her lips; Von who was letting her own bird bones dissolve, letting the pastis do that: this Von was saving a starfish. She plucked it from the pebbles and stumbled into the water, dipped her arms in the froth, then stood and watched as the creature must have gathered its own arms, swum away.

Rebu comes to his table now, leathery face in the strong light. What will you have for lunch today, with the pastis? Mussels again? Bouillabaisse?

Urchins.

Yes, he thinks when the old man's gone back to the kitchen. For Von. An angry sacrifice to her angry soul so she will stay out of his dreams tonight.

When the urchins arrive he eats them fiercely and drinks not one pastis but three, for Von. He eats and drinks and sweats and blinks in this staggering hot light. This has been his table for a dozen years, and he has always wanted the sun, he's thrown open his chest to the sun, he is Mediterranean man and thrusts a fist at the sky to be near it! But today the sun's too bright; his neck and back and wrists are slick, and there's a tremor in his hand.

When the food is gone from his plate, he feels not full but hollowed. And Tino is asking what?

Are you sure? the boy says, face blurring.

Sure what?

That you won't go to Venice? That I should take the project?

Le G wipes his forehead with a stinking napkin. Haven't I already said so? I have no desire to go. Just give it to Amadeo; he's expecting it Monday. I'm too tired, there's too much work.

Too much work?

Yes, yes.

A new project I haven't heard about yet?

No!

Why is he being such a brute to this boy? He's drunk too much. No. Something else.

Drawings, Le G says, paintings. Nothing to tell or show.

This at least is true. Back to these women, three figures on a plane. And a new painting that says to hell with that problem: just a woman, a boat, a shell.

Do you imagine that all three of us can live so close together down there in your seaside fantasy?

Marguerite. Telling him this that awful rainy day in that Paris hotel when he'd been sure she'd give him not just a check but a promise, and instead she'd snapped shut her purse, kissed him on the head, and walked away.

But what was she talking about, three women down here? Herself and Von, all right, but who else?

He stands too quickly from the table, and the sea wavers, and the sky, and Tino's troubled face, a smear.

The doctor, Rebu is saying, I wonder if we should call

Tino is staring at him, but at least his face has settled back to form. As has the sea, the cliff. All have returned. If you stand still and stare, obstinate, these things will return, you can make them go where they belong. When Tino hurries ahead to open the gate for him, he presses his palms to his eyes, salty sour.

That wasn't about three women, only two. When Marguerite said that, looking at him in the Hotel Lutetia. Herself and Von.

This confusion . . . It feels as though something inside him has tilted, sediments have slipped up, clouding.

Where are my bones?

He does not give a damn about dreams!

Oh yes he does. He believes in lurking logic, the courses of undersea currents.

HE STALKS TO THE CABANON, STRIPS, AND STEPS INTO HIS SAGGING black swimming pants. Damned if he won't swim. He'll swim whenever he likes! He climbs back up the concrete steps, left past the fish place and holiday shed and villa, then down the path through the sticky pine trees, the screaming cicadas.

In the cove are two pink bikini girls beneath a striped umbrella; near them, a boy, stretched like a dog on the pebbles. The dog has an eye on the girls. Le G will not bother.

No: the boy has an eye on Le G, and a camera.

Look at the girls! Le G shouts.

The boy smiles and adjusts his lens.

Fine, thinks Le G. Catch the old legend at swim.

He drops his towel, sets his glasses upon it, shoves off his sandals, limps over the hot gray stones to the water. Here they are made new, gleaming, clocking wet underfoot. A few steps in water and he's up to his knees, the old scar numb around his thigh, and finally his feet reach soft sinking sand, and the seafloor drops like a shelf. *Architect-sculptor-swimmer-diver!*

But when he looks out at the sparkling blue, there's a sudden pull of homesickness, as if the sea is not *here.*

He shakes his head. Poises, lunges, crashes in.

He strokes through the water, face under, face up, salt and hot sun, legs kicking and flailing.

Water holding him: its luscious coolness. The first time he

swam in the sea—forty-five years ago? Green water parting to his hands, and, god, the pleasure. Out at that place what was it called not here that first time but the Atlantic, yes, Arcachon, sitting in the dunes drinking then charging into the sea in the dark and letting it hold him and realizing this life, this life, was what he most wanted.

You must see the place I'm building by the sea

He strokes, water sloshing into his gasping mouth. Up to the right: severe cliff with the cave and shaggy greenery, and behind, his tamarisk and cabin and workshop, and the villa.

You should see our place by the sea

That fellow Bado

He was the one yes who said that

What a narrow prison you have made for me

What a narrow prison he'd made?

Yes he said that when Le G was here working, when he'd brought a team from the office to charette for a week, Bado must've given him the keys and had the sense to clear out. Just after the War because first Le G had been here taking care of his murals, and the one downstairs by the sandbox had made him shiver when he saw it, bullet holes all over (executions), and he'd stood before it thinking, Don't repair, no, better to keep the holes as monument, my *Guernica*. Yes, my *Guernica*, no matter what that fart Pablo would say about my painting, condescending old fart. Bullet holes in the mural made the house even better because now part of true life rough life not the barren white thing it had been. Yes now it really lived! Narrow prison? And did Bado say something about a *correction*? Wanting a correction? Remove his paintings, this monument, this museum? Well easy to make short work with a pen, so he sent swift cruel words to

Bado, would publish them too, *Perhaps I misunderstand the sense of your thoughts, as, even though you have lived in Paris for thirty years, you have not yet been able to make others comprehend your writing.* Yes, publish this, why not make this affair public, how that gypsy Bado disdained Le G's enrichment, his gift to sterility. (Sterile bodies sterile house.) But it was unfortunate that after this little contretemps he could no longer stay in the villa, oh but there were rocks and pines aplenty nearby and any little shack would do, even better with goats and chickens, the natural life of Mediterranean man! Which is what he was always, and it was good old Rebu who'd helped (Le G claps at the water with a hand now in applause as he looks up at the fish place), Rebu who'd just put up his restaurant above the white villa, a shack and terrace with grilled fish and cold white wine, looking out at the sea. Urchins, pastis, Tino as a boy standing at Von's knees singing, and all of this was pure life, the life he should have, the life he would have, and all it took was a trade, an original Le G mural for Rebu to elevate his fish shack, a joyous painting of an octopus and party of fish, in exchange for what? His smile was so wide and strong the night he spoke to Rebu, not long after that obnoxious letter from the gypsy, *A correction from you seems necessary*, how preposterous, when what he'd done was made a gift, Le G and Rebu standing beneath the sparkling dark sky and above the sparkling scalloped cove and lapping sea, his hand grasping the other's shoulder.

A mural in exchange for what?

Oh, only a narrow strip of land. Just beside the villa.

Enough space for oh a little building or two.

A house is not only a machine to live in

But an excellent tool for punishment.

A cabanon for you, my love, he said to Von, having drawn it on a napkin in minutes.

And in half a year it was there: 1952. Come, my dear, he said to Von, pulling her into the small dark square smelling of fresh wood and ants. Three strides to one shutter, and it was drawn back to let in a zig of light and color: yellow planks on the floor, blue panels overhead, red curtained toilet. All as compact as the cabin in a zeppelin or aboard ship.

Von teetered on heels at the center. You will make me live in this little place?

He laughed and spun her to see toilet then bed then sink then table: one balletic twirl at the center and the place was embraced entire, its simple elements set like a pinwheel. They'd go down all August, get off the train or park the Fiat and carry their bags to the cabin, shed clothes, work and sweat and swim, drink and eat at the fish place. Sun, sea, rocks, and air! Seeping into his skin, himself seeping into those elements. All that he'd done since the great rip at his life's midpoint had been an ever greater striding into nature, the green and rough and shaggy. In his yearly books he'd chronicle it, his projects, himself in the sand, striding shadow huge in a safari jacket, pockets full of pencils shells pebbles and pinecones. Eating only muscled animals. *There is nothing feminine about him.*

But just now, in the water, good god, something glides past, a quick cold line at his leg, and he gasps and sputters and gropes for his thigh to see if the skin's been sliced free. Only a ray. Its mottled wings glide off, vanish, and he's left panting, barely afloat.

A HALF HOUR LATER HE TRUDGES OVER THE PEBBLES, SALT POWDERing his skin and the hairs on his arms, his smell strong as he reaches for the pole at the boulder, grunts, pulls himself up to the path. How heavy he is, lungs too weak for the air inside them, as if the bellows will collapse. And the light's dull now, the sea gray and forbidding.

When he steps into the cabin and shuts the door, the hollow darkness is almost too much. Open the shutters again: at least the dimness outside is a relief.

He stands at the window and breathes hard, forcing away the weight in his ribs. Pulls off the wet swimsuit, moves to the center of the cabin, raises his arms. An old Renaissance man, inscribing a small cube of space. From the peg he pulls his trousers and hoists them on.

Copying Pablo. Big old man with barrel chest and pants roped at waist like a sailor. Fraud.

Guernica.

To hell with it.

IN THE WORKSHOP, LE G SITS ON HIS WHISKEY CRATE, DRAWING, sipping pastis. One sheet of trace taped atop another, the lines of the figures adjusted a few centimeters until he can finally, finally, get the damned arrangement right. Near him: the fur-covered book, the tiny pelvis bone, the snapping jaw, and a scallop shell. The shell has been his emblem, along with his thumbprint; he presses the shell into the wet concrete of each building as his signature. The scallop's crisp imprint makes clear the point about the concrete building, that it is formed of liquid and not hewn from stone: that it is wholly *made.*

Shells and carapaces.

Shells are like bones.

Where are my bones?

Well, right here, he thinks. Look at my projects, documented here in this inquisitor's book! The church, monastery, housing complexes, villas, embassies, entire damned cities!

These are my bones, what I'll leave behind. To hell with this rank warm meat, old heart muscle and black twist of intestines and even my bad little pet; only the bones will matter. My skull, a femur, a rib in the sand.

The best of me.

In fact, the only fine part.

Like a Parthenon, clean form and light.

a row of white columns in blue

you are a Parthenon to me

He looks out the window, toward the villa.

His feet bare and dirty on the tile floor that night

He wipes his face, smearing soot.

In a moment he again takes up the pencil. Pull the lead along a thigh, smudge the knee, then up the inner thigh. Shift the form of the woman on the right slightly to the left, and extend her arm just enough that its contour is shared by the shin of the other woman, and move the hip of the third one down

He will never get this right!

A spasm of rage jerks him to his feet, and he goes to the shelf, pours another pastis, lets burning licorice puddle his tongue.

Why is he drinking like this? For Von?

Ridiculous. He just wants to.

He turns his head sharply, tacked trace paper wavering in the breeze, the lamplight skidding, bright blur.

He's sick. Worms in his head. Rats in his chest.

He switches off the lamp, staggers to the cabin, feels his way around the entry, falls onto the bed.

Soon he's snoring, heavy and drunk, and this drunkenness plagues him again with poisoned dreams. For now he stands again naked on tiles, cut as he once was by knives drawing out meters of varicose veins and by the propeller blade tearing his thigh, and in his hand as he stands bleeding is a brush. Outside, wind and whipping rain, Marguerite like a sail ripped free flying over the ocean. In the squall, the knocking of heels on stone, but he must concentrate on painting, on the slashes of pink on the wall. He stares into the pink paint as something there moves, splits open, slips out of the wet—

11

WEDNESDAY

Eileen wakes hot in cool gray, reaches for the lever, cranks it until blue sky fills the disk, glad that she can still control this, how the sun shines upon her.

She ponders her circle of sky. What color would it seem to be if I didn't know? If I framed it with fingers and screened away context?

Greenish.

But these eyes and their proclivities.

Eye.

Eye for an

Smoke slowly spirals up the invisible flue.

Anyway now (rolling to her side, crushing out the cigarette, pulling free the nightie tangled between legs, hoisting self on elbow), up on your feet and over the tiles (getting chalky, such dry air up here). Then up the two steps and out the sliding glass door to the terrace.

Feeling sweaty, testy.

Why not swim.

Yes. Why not.

What a morning what a lark fresh as if issued to children

Somewhere in the bag is a swimsuit.

It is August after all, what one does in August.

At Menton, the wide public beach?

No, she thinks. I want my old cove. Just go down there. It's about time.

Swim as you used to every morning into October when you were building the villa, the water clear and no one else there, wavelets washing through pebbles, floating, gazing up.

Eye for an

She sits on the side of the bed and pulls off her nightie, pulls on the swimsuit, threading shanky shins through holes, wiggling to get the thing over her bottom, and then start again threading hands through. So strange how this body is the same but replaced bit by bit, look at the whorls at knees, the saint-thin feet, knobs at big toes. How can I be the same body? What can it mean, some essential body of me? But here we are standing and clad in a black one-piece, still smart, legs and arms still strong enough, even if thin and skin loose, if a shake in the hands, a shake in the head, the bit of stoop in the back. Strong enough. To go where I want.

Wrapper draped over shoulders, straw hat, bathing cap rolled inside towel clamped between elbow and waist, and down the narrow concrete steps (I made these steps) (not strictly true, had Roattino make them). Oh dear, there's mail: must remember to collect it when I return. Across the road to Totor 2. Inside, hot air already this early, yes sticky hot leather seat, then bang of the door and off we go to the beach, down the winding road past the gorge to the right and on through Menton and yes we will refuse to go to that wide public beach but past it and over the small cape.

Yes she'll go exactly where she likes. Will park up near the Rq train station, quite a few cars here but there's a spot—

She races for it with another driver, but her foot's hard on the pedal, can't stop her, oh but they can both fit, can give each other a cold smile, as the other driver, old lady too, climbs from her car as beaten as Totor 2, a bag of greens over her arm, and stands a moment with a hand shielding eyes looking at Eileen.

Does she think she knows me? Old lady carrying a bag with greens spilling out, but as we've seen marketing is something I do not do, so I don't think I know her.

Will take the steep narrow steps down at this end, not the other steps, not the ones by the house, a proper distance from the house. Won't walk left down the path that leads past the old gaudy villa, the only thing around here back when I came that day along the tracks with my stick. Anyway not that way, but down the steps here on this side of the cove, the western side. Down these steep narrow steps clutching the iron rail with towel tucked at elbow, and look at the bougainvillea climbing down the earthen terraces, that color, magenta, fuchsia, oh what's the right name, and what is the small blue trailing flower, can never remember, and the agaves the eucalypts the marvelous fresh scents, and all this is why I came here to build

No, stay focused. On these steps that have at last reached the pebbled cove, good thing you've got on the sturdy rubber sandals, off we go over the clacking pebbles toward that lovely sea. Pebbles hard, feet rolling a little and aching but never mind, this is far enough, towel unfurled, smoothing, so pebbles less hard under tailbone.

And at the idea of her tailbone meeting, but for a sheath of skin and towel, those other pebbles, she thinks, I am geological.

Perhaps ossifying after all. Ah those mountains! Those mountains chipped away over eons and the chips rolled in rivers to the sea and now here, smooth rounded pebbles at my tailbone.

Stop thinking, dissolve, let senses do everything. Just listen now, yes close your eye.

Sun-sparked darkness inside the lid.

Above and behind, a train rattles by rattles by rattles

and is gone, just the cicadas again rising

And a wave crashes upon pebbles, rushes through pebbles, washes back to sea, pebbles clattering clicking quiet

Beneath palms, beneath bottom and feet, the hard stones

Bridge of nose feeling bright in the sun. Chest, too.

Smell of salt, seaweed, fish

Open eye and the sudden wild sear of light

Squint, look close, look at these pebbles. Gray, black, white. White lines in gray, rings cutting through them, pinstripes, how on earth does that happen, a clear stripe of white for instance zigging across that one, is it quartz?

And cockleshells here and there.

silver bells and cockleshells

All right, swim.

Wearing bathing cap makes you sleek. Hard not to feel for an instant your head with the black hair cropped close the fine-tipped curl at your ear back when you were oh forty and the grand robes you'd wear and fine leather boots swishing around Paris with Damia glamorous ladies arm in arm and the cat

The things that just won't die in one's head.

Now up again one two three and keep the rubber sandals on they work well in the water yes let's lurch over the pebbles until they're not chalky but black and wet.

Water, ah. Flowing into sandals, a few slippery steps more and now push off, let go of earth, plunge as you always have, give yourself up to the sea with your legs kicking, pure pleasure to be held like this in water, so voluptuous, the most wonderful feel. Now deep enough beyond tug of wavelets, deep enough to swim properly, and you've always been good at this an athletic girl from the start even before you did such things as ride a camel (yes) drive an ambulance (not quite athletic but nevertheless) pilot a biplane (yes). Water was the first love, the first to hold you and let you let yourself go.

Tread a moment and look at the coast, the cliffs against blue, and beneath them banyans, pines, palms, araucarias, pittosporums, eucalypts, yuccas, oleanders, tamarisks, and on and on it goes, the splendor of plants gathered here! Brought here most of them but so willing to grow! Cedars, umbrella pines, blue morning glories: the extravagance could make you weep.

Swim

Face in water and slash arm and turn face to sun and slash arm and face in and slash arm and kick until after a time must pause, must tread for a spell, catch breath.

And now of course comes the moment that's been in the forecast all morning.

She looks at the house.

Just the sight of it hurts the chest.

And it's not just her house up alone on the rocks, the white deck, blue-and-white awning, glass spiral, and everything that she knows by heart, not just this, aching, but now the chaos around it, everything that man put around it, and why he did she will never know.

Desire for the place or just to punish?

She will never know.

And if she did, what then?

Because even when they managed to throw him out (Bado heroic at last) he hadn't really left, having ruined the house with those paintings. Bado wouldn't paint over them and she wouldn't come back until they were gone.

But they give the house value, Bado kept saying.

Oh value!

Yes, he said, you must see that they link your work and his, in history

You're lovelorn is what you are, she said, living in a shrine to that man a shrine made of my house

I'd like to see you do it yourself, then. Come down with primer and a roller

But she was it's true a coward and proud, a proud coward, and didn't do it either.

And though the man himself had been evicted he managed to lurk. He's always here, Bado said on the phone, he's down at the shoemaker's hut near the water, you know the one little shack at the edge, or up at the fish place that's gone up you know behind the house, and there I am, said Bado, working on the terrace, and when he and Von are at the fish place, I hear his voice, that cawing, he does it for effect, calculating how far it can be heard. And if I look from the terrace up to the fish place, there his glasses are shining in the dusk staring back at me.

But what does he want?

(To punish.)

Then he made his move: got the land next to the fish place, talked the old man there, Rebu, into selling it so he could

Build?

Build, Bado said when he came up to Time one of those hot days to bring her news for a brandy soda. Yes, he's building, he said, as he ran a hand through thin hair and looked over her patio and into her glass doors. Building a cabin.

A cabin?

I've heard he calls it a primal abode for natural man. Not talking to me of course anymore, but I heard.

Where?

Right next to the house.

But why there?

Don't know, lots of lots elsewhere.

A primal abode for natural man?

Taking possession of space is the first gesture of living things, of men and

Then the cabanon emerged (she studied the drawings in his latest *oeuvre complète*, not ashamed to admit it): a cube of rough logs, tiny entryway a muraled slot to step around before reaching the single small room, and oh, just look: it was organized by an invisible spiral, a kind of pinwheel design, toilet then bed then sink then table appearing in neat rotation. And the furniture all built in.

Ha ha.

Insulting flattery.

But after that, and she sees it now, floating on her back, watery depths holding up her bones, fingertips just beginning to prune. She sees it as a blur of images of Bado dragging himself up her steps with news, each time more thin, more gray. What he's done now, Bado said, groping behind himself for a chair, he's started to use another shack, little plank thing for working, two windows facing the sea and not just the sea, he said, laughing, exhausted. He looks right into the bedroom. There I am swinging around undressed, and there he is, can see that head looking right at me.

And then, Bado said, his skin seeping into his white shirt, sitting waiting for the drink he shouldn't have but needed (he had one of those redheads or blondes living down there with him, doing him no good). Passing him the drink, Eileen's hand was thin and spotted, and Bado's hand was thin and trembling, but the glass was just as it had been back in the twenties, when first she handed it to him in Paris and he looked at her with besotted satyr eyes. Touching a fingertip to the side of his mouth he said, Now on top of the fish place that he's tarted up and painted, on top of his own little cabin and the shack beside it, now he's planning to do a whole village of holiday houses, hundreds of them, an army of goblins painted those damned bright yellow red and blue, climbing up the hill.

How does he finance this?

Oh one of those secret ladies of his, rich American wouldn't you know, one of those women he meets in hotels and sends cards with little drawings and they write back to him at his office so Von won't know, she's the one who's funding this, her name's something like Margaret.

But then apparently, E learnt, a monsoon came and knocked out the idea of that vast holiday village. Even up in the vineyards everything shook and rocked, wind howling under the louvers, the ceiling eye nearly sucked from its socket, and Eileen lay there worrying about the house down on the rocks and Bado in it gray and weak and his silly blond woman not helping, the place shuddering, water rising, waves slashing over the terrace and in.

So that was the end of this part of Le Grand's coup, the hillside of holiday houses, for the rich lady must have thought better of the investment and pulled out. But he still made one little set of them, a shed of little holiday rooms, right behind the villa: you could practically touch them.

Her place surrounded.

Then the frantic feeling started, and the calls with Bado, E saying, We've got to sort it out, now, the title to the house, the deed, because who knows what that man might try to do, we've got to make sure the house is in my name.

But Bado by then was not well enough to drive up or meet and said, Don't worry, I'll get together the documents.

But months passed and nothing, then he was off on a trip again, oh those big architect men so alluring, but he couldn't manage the trip, too sick, had to get off the ship, turn back: rot creeping from his liver. She called the hospital and arranged to come the next day to be with him after surgery. But when she did and found his room, a nurse looked up and said, I'm sorry, and the bed was already stripped.

SHE'S CHILLED NOW FROM THE WATER. KICKS HERSELF IN, LETS A wave help, crawls through shallows on hands and knees upon the bruising pebbles.

She ended up burying Bado alone. All those parties, those weekends, no one there, not even the blonde. Although the old goat wrote a sort of obituary, getting just about everything wrong.

AND NOW THAT SHE'S BACK ON HER TOWEL, ON THE PEBBLES, OLD starfish gazing into the deep blue, she will do it calmly.

She turns and looks straight at her house. Up on the dark rocks, elegant, shy.

It still feels just like herself.

The last time she was there, ten years ago, they were to meet, that blond woman and she, at half past eleven. With Bado gone she didn't have the heart at first, not for some months, but finally wrote to that woman, saying she needed the keys. She came early so there would be no mistake. Walked back and forth along the path above the gate (locked). A place she'd pulled from the ground (love!).

The woman Mireille or Mirabelle turned up half an hour late. Plump with soft hands and frizzed hair and slippery brown eyes. Make short work of this, E thought. Let's go.

The keys, please, she said. I'll be moving back to my house.

Keys? Back?

The woman claimed to have no keys, yet then produced them, yet would not hand them over, and ran down the steps and through the gate and along the path to Eileen's front door. And there she stood, saying, I've no reason to think you have anything to do with this place. Have you a title? A deed?

AND THAT WAS THE END. THE END OF EILEEN'S HOUSE BY THE SEA. Standing humiliated on her own steps.

She shuts her eyes and folds arms over her chest, cold in her swimsuit in the Mediterranean sun.

Or that was almost the end. A few more moments, but enough.

She sits, gathers her towel and hat and keys, and with a cold wet hand clutching the rail, climbs the concrete steps up to the path, to the train station, the car park.

THAT EVENING AFTER A SCANT DINNER OF BREAD, OLIVES, AND cheese, and a drink or two too many, she looks at the blur of starry wild sky and feels herself slip, start to fly from her throat.

Yes do something.

Must.

But what.

Behind her tousled silver head, inside the sliding glass doors, inside the second house she built but had to leave, there's a sudden rummage of ghosts. Men burn her drawings and snap off chair legs and throw them into the fire, go through her drawers and pull out pajamas sad old pajamas! and tromp them with muddy bloody boots

12

WEDNESDAY

Not a dream! Le Grand bolts up at a creak, sees a foot stepping from the wall.

I'm sorry, she says. But you didn't hear me knock so

What?

It's time, and she pulls the needle from her apron.

Ah.

He falls back. Almost laughs but the ache in his ribs makes him stop.

Monsieur?

Madame Rebu, he says, clutching at his chest, I'm sorry.

You are well?

No oh no, I'm old.

You have a pain?

I have always had pain, always, always, I am the octopus beaten on rocks.

Ah yes. She draws liquid from the vial, eyes it in the light. Turn, please. You know how we do this.

He laughs, weak, and rolls over to give his rump to the stab of her needle. Then lies still, the horror of his dream roiling through him. Something alive in these walls pressed inside the wood scratching out

Such a sense of things all wrong. Of *being* wrong, himself.

WHEN MADAME REBU IS GONE, HE PUSHES HIMSELF UP, AND GOD how everything hurts, the damned pastis and rats in his ribs and deep bone ache of these shots. He goes outside with the coffee she left and can hear his own breaths thick and damp, feel his heart move inside his chest, twitching old primordial slug.

So bright out, the sun already high, must be nearly ten, blinding, debilitating, and how can this be when he has always thrived in strong sun? Squinting, shielding eyes with a hand, he looks now beyond the glass spiral atop the villa and beyond the fish place to the roof of the holiday shed.

So cheerful they'd been, so hopeful, a sign that he'd have everything, with Von and Marguerite and his three skinny pine trees and four square meters of sand, but then everything turned, a year of darkness. Marguerite would have had the choicest cabin. What a dream! In a single stroke he'd have a village of his design and the woman he most wanted in bed only a few paces away! But then came the rainy day at the Hotel Lutetia when she said, Do you really imagine that the three of us can live so close together? That you can walk up the path when Von is sleeping, slip into my cabin, disappear at dawn, and that this can go on and on? Yes. He had imagined exactly that. He hadn't bothered thinking of daylight, how fantasy shrivels. And when Marguerite snapped her purse and kissed him on the head like a baby and left, that had been the start of chaos, the turn downward as if the pinnacle of his life had been reached and now came the sign to heaven or hell to break forth and not only take the project but threaten his whole precious enclave, torrents and waves sloshing up at the earthen terrace. Then Von, too, finally slid away. By then he could barely stand her up on the floor before she'd giggle drunk and tumble, legs broken thrice, sugar sticks. How many times had he picked her up, placed her in a chair, and fed her meat and milk to make her bones strong? How many times, here and in Paris? It's all blurred, years of it, but still clear is the cold green light on the last day in the hospital. The cold smell of the room, sketching her as he sat by her bed, nothing else he could do after stroking her arm (bone) her face (bone). Then drawing her face, the pencil's lead, the soft dry strokes of pencil meeting her breath, strange quiet communion.

Her breaths coming less, less, less, no more.

Returning alone.

Spaces doubly empty, Von not in their rooftop flat in Paris so must be down in the cabin, then not in the cabin either.

And soon after Von, his mother.

Then everything collapsed, the yellow and blue and red rooms, hominess of Von and holiness of Mother and that secret space of fleshly women, Marguerite above all.

So could you blame him if in desperation at Von's funeral he grasped for something comforting, plunged his hand into the vat of ash and plucked from it a little bone?

So alone then, so alone, rattling around, scraped bare.

And somewhere in this chaos, Bado, who'd always been slithering just out of sight, in all of this he was gone, too.

Yes. He'd written the man's obituary himself.

It somehow took a day or two for Le G to realize that with Bado gone, the white villa was abandoned.

So could you blame him if, in desperation, being adrift and alone, he clutched for the white house on the rock?

Now, too, as he thinks all this, he needs comfort.

Here is Von's bone, in his pocket where he tucked it last night. He fingers it gently, its curves familiar, pulls it out to look at, not just hold it, but look: a small thing in itself.

Brittle, tiny piece of her pelvis.

The names he once knew

Sacrum, ilium.

The words are so lovely: like names of a holy place.

He looks at the bone in his palm.

But it *had* been a holy place.

For the first time he feels ill, seeing this. Once alive and hidden inside his lonely wife.

He can't work today. He doesn't even want to swim, too heavy and compacted for that.

Not down, then. Up.

Yes, up to see Von.

I'm taking your car! he yells to Rebu as he passes the fish place, and walks quickly up the path through eucalypts, cicadas, pines. In the small lot by the train station, he swings open the door, finds the key under the seat, still warm, climbs in.

Much better. Motion. Foot heavy on pedal and the stink of fuel and vibrations in hands. Up the steep narrow road, over and along the gorge, then the hairpins that lead sickening up and up to the ancient town, the sea far and hazy.

Up there to the cemetery, to the delicate monument he made for Von and himself on the edge, dizzyingly high, you can feel the world spinning from here, spinning beneath your feet. He crouches, touches both small urns, no higher than his knees. A concrete prism waits for him with a tablet of yellow, blue, and red; a slim concrete cylinder with a gold cross holds her.

Von.

Suddenly he is a large, heavy, ramshackle man crouching, glasses greasy, strands of white-iron hair askew, feet atop the boxed ash of his wife.

Vonny, Yvonne. What had she been? A shopgirl, a model. He'd plucked her from that and made her a beautiful aerie in Paris, top of the building, roof garden, but alone. From up there you could look far down at the street. How terrible could it have been? She had so few hours to get through each day! He'd wake her at eight-thirty with coffee, and already by five he was home again, for pastis. From her high bed, the high bed he'd made her, she could lie all day if she wanted and stare over the outskirts of Paris to the west, the low hills, the yellow skyline. In the kitchen, cooking bouillabaisse, she could stare out the narrow cold window at the slot at the heart of the building, at the spikes to keep away birds. She had nothing to do but face each hour and let it pass through her, and then came the next, just wave after wave of time passing through her—how hard could it be? When he was in Paris, anyway. When he was not in Paris, well, he could not know what she did. He asked friends to go over, of course, to look in. He wrote her daily. She wrote him. She wrote his mother. She drank her pastis at noon, or for breakfast. She fed the sparrows: he knows that. And named them, too, those hundreds of sparrows that would flock to their rooftop garden, where she would stand, a handful of seed.

She had been a model, that's how he'd found her. Lifted her

and placed her up in that aerie, kept her safe. That's what he had wanted to do, keep her safe.

Madame begs me for children, he told that Indian journalist. *I have no desire whatever for children.*

Yet when he said that, he and she were already sixty? What was he thinking?

Searing visions of young Von kneeling above him in bed, weeping, saying, When will we be legal, will we ever be legal? And again, after those shameful years, her weeping, saying, Of course it's too late now, no child, so what am I to do, then? Why have you got me?

And then, of course, what he did all night with that lady journalist. Or wanted to, anyway: just now he can't remember. *I like my women fat.* If not her, a dozen others.

Insatiability. Is that what it was? One woman and another. What was it he'd needed? What was insatiability, anyway? A hollowness. A hollowness that only grew deeper the more it was fed. A hunger, a need, for what?

And what is the need that moves in him now? An animal muscle craves to plunge into mud, to sink.

Maybe something like Von, after all. Didn't she pour liquor into herself with a terrible lust not to *be*?

He's brought birdseed with him. The best he can do. He grunts, knees creaking as he rises and pulls the little bag from his pocket. He opens it, sprinkles the seeds on her circle.

And stands there, looking at the black specks.

As if they might sprout wings.

A wriggle of life just then inside him. A wriggle of pain. Back to the car, hurry, drive fast.

THAT NIGHT, HIS HALF-AWAKE DREAMS ARE ALL SWIMMING IN blackness that's ink or liquid ash or fur, the tips of Pinceau's ears. It's all swimming through black water, parting it, being enveloped. His hands press against rock, press in, into soft living rock? Does he plunge his self in, as he's longed to? Plunge himself into it and *be* it, be gone?

Oh, the diver, and his tomb. Tomba del Tuffatore. Hundreds of miles around the coast from Cap M, to the east and then south, in Italy. A boy dives, painted on the upper slab of a tomb, painted two and a half thousand years ago, by a Greek with his brushes and pots of paint. The boy's the rich color of terra-cotta but for his black hair and brow and the clear white of his eye. He's nude and dives with poise, fingers pointing forward, toes tight behind, tiny penis brave in the air. One spare tree waves him forward, another waves from behind, as he plunges toward a tossing green sea, a watery way to the underworld.

Below this slab the tomb's occupant lies gazing up at the diver, maybe himself, diving one last time.

13

THURSDAY

From the terrace Eileen can see not only over the valley to the haze of Mediterranean but across the road to where men work in the vineyard. What are they up to now? (Binoculars.) Removing green bunches of grapes, exactly as I hope they're now doing at home, too.

Flowers on the vines need no bees, she'd been happy to learn, for they fertilize themselves.

Parthenogenesis

And with that old word comes the tired old memory

And what honestly would she do, what she let herself see in a dream?

Doors kicked in, matches struck, flames

But visions like that: no. Quite calm in daylight. Back to one's civilized self.

She swerves the binoculars close, everything enormous down on the road, and here comes the old couple. Still nine paces apart, she in front determined, he behind bobbing his head left and right. Different headgear today, though, he in an old gray hat and she in a red scarf. She looks furious, nose-first marching up the hill, he wandering with his stick. Maybe there's a paradox here. Who is it, Zeno, a paradox about perpetual distance, of two beings yoked but always with space between.

Binoculars down, Eileen walks to the other end of the terrace near the trumpet flower and gangway and thinks, Maybe I'm missing an obvious point in extending this house, maybe another bridge would be right. Artist Graham has an artist wife, too, and though he didn't say so, she suspects this extension will let them abide together longer. So perhaps a bridge (gangplank) after all, à la hyphenated villa, like Romaine and Natalie built, and like that place of Frida and Diego's, and in a way something like Charles and Ray's with that space between halves, my haven't I known a lot of famous people. So maybe yes a hyphenated house, as the extra rooms will be for one of the two, I should think, never having managed to live (happily) with anyone myself, nor knowing an artist who could, and a pair of artists compounds the problem, so perhaps a bridge, a hyphen.

What he thought he was doing, building his house by mine?

She stands still, ponders her hands.

Well, we can all think what we like.

LATE AFTERNOON: A VIGOROUS DAY AT LAST. JUST LIKE HER OLD (young) self again. Big drawings on sheet after sheet and enough noting and sketching for there to be something to show, concrete enough to give Graham two solid ideas from which they might proceed, with and without the hyphen. Good.

Curious: even though she's been more engaged with the house today than since she arrived, studying surfaces and volumes and sketching possible changes, she's actually been the most able to detach self from house, imagine it having a future without her, and doesn't this feel fine.

Levitation.

So that—pausing on the terrace again, leaning on the rail and looking over the glorious green and ochre and blue, and it is an extraordinary situation here, where the Alps crash into sea—when a car passes below raising a hot ghost of dust, she does not, for once, see Bado.

Some putrefy, others ossify

Or purify.

She shuts her eyes (eye), tilts head back for full sun on face, and feels nineteen, can feel herself at nineteen, wearing a party of a hat with her masses of dark hair piled up and in a full-skirted silk dress cinched at the waist and a smart tiny jacket and gloves, how far away, and she was a luscious one with her pale far-apart eyes and small smile and splendid figure. Yes she is still that self and all the selves between, that young bedecked girl and then the one with short black hair in a black silk suit vamping with Jessie in her mustache and later with Damia one hand holding the leash, and later versions too how glorious when you think of it she's like an insect's compound eye all those tiny selves inside! Or how women are born with all the eggs they'll ever have. But anyway glad not to be a usual woman but otherwise. And, besides, she's still here, almost the only one of her set walking the earth, and she feels grand, elevated, so guess what? She'll take herself to dinner. Up to the fancy place way up high, what's it called, La Turbie.

A fortifying dinner, ceremonial.

Ideas always swirl within her until at last they settle enough she can see what to do.

And tomorrow yes she'll ask Pruny to come.

Can't get dressed up enough as didn't bring fancy things, but never mind, just a brooch and scarf and withering look at anyone from the one visible eye, must never forget the blackened glass and its startling effect. Down the concrete steps, oh to be going out in the evening! In Totor 2 driving down past the gorge and into Menton (gassy, honking, bare legs, bright short dresses, polka dots, stripes) then along Menton's wide beach, skirting the cape, past the ancient olive grove, past the house by the sea, can't see it now but soon enough, yes, and away from the coast and climbing again, cemetery high to the right, then onward upward past ancient Rq with its castle and steep cobbled roads, and farther along the corniche, grinding upward, don't get dizzy when you glance over that shocking expanse of sea, little Monaco way down there, this view so famous now in movies, convertible on cliff, starlet in scarf, of course you won't get dizzy not you who piloted an airplane! Up to the village of La T, topped by the Roman ruin, trophy that Augustus made for lording it over the tribes of the Alps, a thing you can see for miles.

Park and let's have a look, a stroll before dining.

She walks up the cobbled road to the ruin's enclosure, a quiet leafy grove. Interesting to find oneself in an altogether different precinct, a place not of this era, a holy or secretive feel, in the early evening air, alone. Then through the grove out to the monument and it's like an acropolis, huge blocks of white limestone against sheer sky, enormous monument two thousand years old at the top of this village at the top of this Alp closest to the sea. Towering even higher from this enormously high spot. Power! A ring of white limestone columns on a plinth, Tuscan, pure, and to look up at their white against the deepening sky is nearly to topple backward. Then she climbs the steps up to the terrace on the plinth and from here can see the blue Mediterranean sliding over the bowl of the globe. Turn one way and it's Italy, the other and it's France, behind and it's the last crest of Alps, then Switzerland and Germany, whence the Alpine tribes Augustus conquered. Celts, Ligurians, though this was their home, this was the Ligurian Sea! Look at that blond girl kneeling in chains on the frieze, look at the shaggy blond boy.

Oh Augustus, you can carve the names of all the tribes you conquered, but they, we, are back. Have a look down at the beaches and you shall see miles of boys and girls just like them.

Waves and waves and waves roll in, as far as she can see

replacing each other, repeating

Let's let waves pass through us a moment, too: waves of light, and sound, and air.

A hawk soars slowly, wings still.

Last long look, all around.

Now back down the steps, to the shadowy grove, just a stray cat and a bowl someone's filled for it, lucky cat. Down the cobbled road to Rue Edward Tuck, and here it is, the monastery.

Which is now, la la, a fine restaurant.

Mademoiselle is alone?

If that's how you'd like to put it, yes. (But if you could hear what goes on between my ears.)

Tablecloths, heavy silver, candles, tender clinks

Look at these delicious choices.

Hot oysters on the half shell with orange butter, or grilled duck breast with pickled cherries, or roast chicken with crayfish butter, or poached langoustine with coriander, or

Her face is lit with orange fragrance, with flame.

14

THURSDAY

When he wakes on the narrow wooden bed, Le Grand feels like a man in the ocean clutching a plank, Odysseus alone in the waves. His old mother underworld, his waiting wife, fabulous whores on their islands: and that other.

The sheets are salty, so is his skin, and he doesn't need to look or touch to know he has an old visitor. Purplish muscle struggles to rise as he lies back helpless, clasps it, then lets it flop between his legs.

Sad old squid.

SOON THERE HE IS AGAIN, BEHIND THE RED CURTAIN. THIS IS WHAT it has come to, a drama like this: old man huddled over a toilet, looking down at a gray thing dangling from a scraggle of fur, as he rocks and strains and squints out the slot of window to the stone that his cabanon clutches.

He feels like a comet that's burned up, the trail of energy

behind him—all that drawing painting building writing talking striding fucking—blasted out now, gone. Who would have thought so much could be in one sack of skin? But now he's nearly done, just an old pile of flesh atop a stinking warm toilet.

Out the slot of window, hot stone.

What is it, sedentary, no, *sedimentary*. But no, this rock is metamorphic, igneous. Can't get harder than that.

Amazing that she'd screwed her house into such rock.

The idea of that woman making a house so supremely simple yet intricate, elegant, around a spiral of stairs, and twisting it into this rock, a house following the sun. A *first* house.

Stunning.

He'd so admired it.

And her. Yes. He'd so admired *her*.

His hands on his knees, grubby nails. The stitches at his fingertip winding around his stout thigh. The ray of skin floating in pink froth, the white boat

Well didn't he do what he had to? First to show his admiration no matter how she mistook it and then to keep the place safe, yes, keep it shored up. That fool Bado had left the place untethered, so he had to step in, go to the town hall, learn that Bado was of course intestate (headless), the blonde removed, the place abandoned, so yes he stepped in and said he'd help, was an old friend, felt a responsibility, and what with his connections he arranged an auction and all right arranged who'd bid highest. He had to. A property of unimaginable value, he'd whispered to Madame S (patroness in the making). This house is one of my darlings, he'd said, so who knew what she thought she'd be getting, what house this was and who'd made it? It *was* one of his darlings. He'd made a model of it he kept on his desk in Paris. An important villa, he'd said to Madame S when he'd first written her in Zurich, a place you might like to own. Forming the hinge between the largest movements in my aesthetic, both the purity and elegance of white wall and floating floors and the primal, the natural.

Look, my dear madame, he'd said when she came down for the auction, if you will let me escort you through this delightfully subtle entryway, how suddenly the sea opens as a bright slash before your eyes, behold, and the shutters so clever they can reveal nothing or slant into slots or dissolve altogether, and the furnishings (dancing her over the tiled floors as he unfolded a shelf, opened a wall, pulled from its hiding place a mirror), the furnishings are the house's vital organs. Even those that stand alone, this marvelous chair with a single Amazonian arm, for instance, and this one conceived as a deck chair so refined, are of the rarest spirit, created to live within this house. For it is a complete being, dwelling between sun and water and stone, as much animal as mineral. Every part of it is brilliant.

To which she smiled and said, Of course it is, this marvelous house, as fine, as brilliant, as everything you make.

Well, he didn't say it; she did. She believed what she wished. He just didn't correct, just nodded with lenses all light, a minor sin of omission.

A correction from you seems necessary

And that was before getting to the main point, the heart of the house: the murals. Integral to the house's spirit. So now his tour became a promenade to see only his paintings (remembers now clearly, with elbows jabbed into knees as he waits on the toilet and looks through the slot at igneous stone and squashed red cactus fruit), and this tour of the house was such keen pleasure, letting him speak of the work no one had ever regarded properly:

his painting. Even as he pointed out each mural and discussed its composition he had a vague double sense of what had been there before, here in the main room something had been designed for the wall, a large collage, was it *Invitation to a voyage*, was that it? He could not recall where it was; had he taken it down and put it elsewhere? But never mind, on with the tour, the third one, the water, blood, propeller.

And at that point to seem the connoisseur she crossed her arms languidly as women do, forming that lissome knot of fragility and strength, cast her face at an appraising angle, and said, Yes, remarkable, these murals are as splendid as the rest of the house, if perhaps in need of

Precisely, he said. So you wouldn't mind if I came around to retouch them?

To which she said, Certainly not, I'd wish for it. You are the genius of this place.

So yes, it's true, he let this happen.

Possession of space is the first gesture of

He feels now something, can almost feel something, like bark closing over his shins.

He sits vacant, hand on a knee. A clod of dirt drops from the rock outside the window; a grass blade stirs.

Then a sudden earthquake within.

It's all he can do to concentrate, hold firm.

Ten brutal minutes later: he's done. Exhausted. He feels the waft of air that will blow this horror out of the cabin, and sits aching and dredged.

Then stands and hoists up trousers, reties the rope, pushes through the red curtain.

Work.

Can't.

Swim.

Can't.

Walk then! Walk in the cove.

THE PINE TREES BREATHE OUT STICKY HEAT, PEBBLES KNUCKLE HIS soft arches as he lurches by the frill of water, old walrus of a man.

He gazes up at the slab of stone, the slim white yacht.

From here, you can't see what he's done to it.

Except, of course, for the cabins and shacks pushing from all sides.

It is indescribably elegant, with its slim legs and band of window. Looking down at this old monster on the shore.

A correction from you seems necessary.

BACK AT THE CABANON, HE GRIPS THE LEDGE AND LEANS OVER THE agave, cranes around to the restaurant terrace.

Rebu!

The elder, he means. His gnome face appears.

Do you remember the name of that woman?

Rebu's face splits into a laugh. Which?

The one who—Le G jabs his head toward the villa—who used to live down there.

The blonde?

Before that.

Red?

No no before all that.

The American?

No, not American. English, maybe.

Will ask my wife.

Le G goes back into the cabin, sits at the little table that wings from the wall, takes his pen and a card from a stack, turns the card over.

Chère mademoiselle.

And?

Chère mademoiselle,

I

What I

I wonder if I

I and I and I and what! He gets up. Bends at the small square window, fist at hip, and stares at the square of world he's created, the square of sky and sea.

Something he needs to do. This emptiness, this craving. It started at the squid but grew inward and upward until now he is filled with it—filled with an emptiness? What sense does that make? But emptiness fills him, and now, breathing slowly, with his breath it comes.

To paint.

HE THINKS: HOW CURIOUS THAT IN TASTES, IN DEEP AESTHETIC convictions, we swing from pole to pole. First the need for whiteness, bone, marble, sloughing off decoration and all that's impure. Then this seems sterile, and we need what is organic, rough, primal, deep bloody colors of body and earth.

And now I go back to where I began, he thinks. Again I long

for what's clean, color burned off, stone after centuries when the paint's worn away, bone bleached dry in the sun.

When the cathedrals were white

He jams swollen feet into sandals, smooths the strands of hair on his head, goes out into the dazzle and cicada scream, and limps up the sweeping arc of steps.

Up the path stands Tino. Why is he always so anxious? Why is he always lurking?

Good morning, he calls out. Where are you off to?

Town.

Please, it's too hot. I'll go for you, just tell me, you need soap maybe or paper

No, I'm going myself.

The boy is flung off like a jacket, left against a pine looking stricken, and there's no way for him to know that this big old man moves forward because a tiny particle of light burns inside him. From outside, as ever, he is *brut.*

My mother wanted me to tell you, Tino calls, about that woman, the one who lived here, she saw her just yesterday

Ah, did she, he thinks. Good. Still up there.

The next train to Menton's in seven minutes. As he stands on the platform the sun seems to melt the skin of his head, his glasses oily in the mercuric air. When the train arrives he pulls himself up from the platform, shocked by his own weight.

He grunts and with a spotted hand shoves away whatever addresses him. Thank god a seat is open right here; he crashes into it. In a moment objects take place around him again: dirty floor, sharp smell of a boy, netted bag of groceries slumped by a woman's shoe. The horizontal strip of sky and sea and green through the window's scratched glass: he fixes his eyes on that, the strip sliding as he glides, the steel rail far beneath his feet but almost something he feels, skating hot. Iron on his head, oiled too; he runs a hand over the strands again, is surprised at the cool wet.

His stop: he manages a better descent than ascent, and thank god where he's going is just two blocks away. He crosses the fuming honking street, veers into the shade, shop fronts bouncing. A grocery, green hair of carrot spilling over a stall, pyramid of lemons, potatoes in dirt. Old bookstore with postcards in boxes outside, and at the sight of them he sees again the casbah girls on those cards long ago, flesh naked but hair jeweled, and he still has them in the shack and will pull them out, he needs them, something still in the arrangement of those women, that damned set of poses he has got to get right because he still hasn't, not in the big black-and-white sgraffito at the villa and not in the dozens of paintings and drawings before and after, and he thinks all this in the time he takes a single step and is overwhelmed as he realizes this, too, the travel he's done in less than a second, back forty years and over the sea, it's a miracle anyone can keep walking.

The hardware store now, its smell of seeds, oil, and iron. But he hasn't thought this through properly. Of course he'll need more than he can carry. He'll only be able to get one on this trip. He'll have the rest delivered tomorrow.

He pays, makes the arrangement, and leaves the store, a can swinging heavy from his hand.

Back at his workshop, he places it by the door. For tomorrow. But first pry it open for ah the smell.

A return to so long ago, the first dazzle of sea, salt, scoured clean.

HE PICKS UP THE CARD HE'D BEGUN ON HIS TABLE. SWIFT WORDS:

Would you be so kind as to visit? Something I'd like no I need to show

Tino can drive it up. Up there to that house, what's it called, Time.

THAT NIGHT, AT THE EDGES OF HIS DREAMING, SEASHELLS SCATTER into the air. Seashells and bottles lift into the sky, their small round mouths open and singing.

There's another diver! Also in a tomb, but joyous. This one's Etruscan, not far from Cap M, clockwise around the coast. Another boy diving, although this boy was painted first. His skin's rich terra-cotta, too, his hair and brow also black. His hands too are pointed, toes behind him held tight. He's diving from a cliff, the different layers of rock different colors, and from the cliff a friend calls, Wait!

But he wanted to dive, was wild to plunge into the purple sea. Fish leap up, a dolphin leaps, too, and all around this diving boy, red and blue and yellow birds soar into the sky.

15

FRIDAY MORNING

Eileen is in the garden under her hat, calmly sketching a plan for the lower terrace that will work with the new structure, bridge, and placement of footings with respect to shadow and what the garden beds will need. She taps a weak branch of an old lemon, mighty tree to have survived those four awful years of looting, peers over the wall to see the vines across the road, then climbs the steps to the gangway. Hand clasping rail, she thinks about the sight of herself and the question of aesthetics, whether the ancient (herself) suits the modern, or no.

Yes. Especially those of us who go back to the bone.

Some putrefy, others ossify

Purify

Pruny should be here tomorrow morning, said she'd set out at dawn.

The bell rings for the post, rings Eileen back to the now.

Post will not be for her, of course, but can't let it jam the box, so down the concrete steps she goes, blinded in the shadows after sun.

Here we are, magazines and so on and what seem to be bills, maybe a letter.

And a postcard

Can't help but look, who wouldn't.

What?

Once she's under the awning, she lets herself look, note the handwriting.

Where is the loupe

And the return address, but oh this can't be

A tiny cartoon of a man in glasses

Chère mademoiselle

She cannot be seeing this.

Chère mademoiselle, if I may presume, I would be pleased if you would be so kind as to visit as there's something I'd like no I need now to show you—

Visit? Now? Something *you* need?

But what on earth is the date?

Yesterday. No stamp. Delivered by hand.

Right here, in this white house on a hill, her drawings and plans once burst into flame.

16

FRIDAY MORNING

To swim!

When Le Grand wakes, it's with a delight that's buoying. Through his shutter-framed square is liquid green, and he's beside himself, outside himself, happier than he's been in months, as though something has been set loose within.

Swim. Architect-sculptor-swimmer-diver! Mediterranean man.

Fifty years slide from his shoulders, and everything he sees and smells makes him wild with pleasure: fine silty soil beneath bare feet as he walks from cabanon to steps, the fresh smell of tamarisk. He nearly runs—and where has this come from, this lightness, this vim?

The concrete is ribbed on the path toward the cove, and he is smitten again with love for the stuff. *Brut.* Of course it is *brut,* it is crude; that is its allure; only a fool would not understand. And anyway there is a fine beauty in it, too, if you must have fineness: look how the concrete holds the grain of a living tree. Like a fossil we can make ourselves.

Here, for instance, on the path beneath his feet as they pace over dry needles: in the concrete here is the impression left by a tire tread, because some fool backed onto the wet surface and left this memento of motion. When a surface speaks and tells of more than its own dimensionless self, what else could you want of the world? It even looks—he thinks as he pauses, towel moist around his neck—the tire tread looks like the back of a crocodile. So this almost *is* a fossil. That the dry and particular can be mixed and made liquid and then given the impression of something alive: how is this not exquisite? That material holds memory in form?

Onward through pines, singing cicadas, down the steps and over volcanic rock to the pebbles. They still keep the coolness and color of dawn. And strange: he barely feels them today, when yesterday they bruised his arches. As if today he truly is light and rare.

Now he reaches the water's frothing edge, steps upon the firm damp sand, and nearly melts at its slight spring, its give.

He is a child at the beach! The desire to sculpt and model with his hands, to dig and make: enormous! The impulse that has driven him always. An itching in palms to print himself upon matter, to form, to mark, to plunge.

He's about to step into the water, but stops and turns to look at the villa.

Correction.

All right then.

For a moment he studies his prints in the sand. Casts of each foot formed by weight, maybe his truest point of contact with this world. No? The large toe, wrinkled instep, and—what he can't see in this sand but knows would be there in fine concrete—whorls. Private patterns made involuntarily yet made by him all the same, more purely so than all he's consciously made. It's true.

Why should these small impressions signify less than the impressions the mind might engineer with concrete? Perhaps it is in this—footprint, handprint—that man is most purely a *faber.*

Face the sea now, fists at hips.

The sandy stretch is a springboard. He bends old knees, drops into a diver's pose.

Architect-sculptor-swimmer-diver!

A sea-lion splash, and he's enveloped in cool. Face under, eyes open to the greenish haze and sting, then up, salt wet running from his mouth as he lashes his head left then right, casts forward, clutching liquid with arms.

Water holding him again: its voluptuousness, his first and greatest pleasure. As if the organ dangling between his legs had only temporarily stood for him in the long midstretch of his life and has finally released its hold, letting pleasure spread all over him as a boy again, brand-new.

Delight

a dolphin splashing in his element

But maybe

Yes

A bit slower.

Odd that in the water he only now begins to feel his flesh again, heavy, when on ground he'd been all air. Knees feel cold. Head to left, head to right. Blurred sunlit cliff, green and rock, sliding away, the harsh sound of breaths, slashing arms, thudding heart. A plume of bitter cold now. Beneath him, deep and black.

Far around the coast, near Marseille, is that underwater cave, where twenty thousand years ago people went with charcoal, shells, and torches, fingers trailing the walls: there are still on the stone their paintings of seals, jellyfish, ibex. A row of horses: their eyes so clear, their manes drawn with combing fingers. Three auks tumbling in waves.

These people left traces of themselves, too. They placed their hands upon the rock, blew red or black pigment around fingers. There!

A child wanted to do it. But let's try something else now: lift her on shoulders, make her tall, yes, so she can leave a mark up high, where the white limestone is soft and wet. In fact it's more than that: it's moonmilk, liquid stone. She can press her hand into living stone.

Hold her knees tight, let her reach—

There!

It happens now: a pain that's blanching.

At first he thinks, *Of course.*

A pain like lightning as it sears his chest, making immaterial the muscle of heart, the rest of his lurching body.

A sense, underwater or above, of white
of being inside a sleeve of white
the skimming underside of a yacht
brilliant slab of Alp
fluted column against blue
From above, through water, fall voices.

WHETHER YOU ADD YOUR OWN MATTER TO THE WORLD OR PRESS yourself into, model that matter: is one more than the other?

VON ON THE COLD ROOF IN PARIS, MURMURING TO SPARROWS, STARing at life far below her feet. Yes. He did that to her. But: far away, another woman on the roof of a huge building gazes with delight across the landscape at the rising sun, a child playing beside her. Le Grand did that, too. And farther, a couple steps into a white chapel where light falls through red, blue, yellow panes of glass, and they are silent with a joy touching holy. And even farther away, a boy slides from his bedroom into a swimming pool. He had always dreamt, he told Le Grand—*always!* a nine-year-old boy!—of waking and somersaulting from his bed to a slide, gliding down to a swimming pool. So Le Grand had made this for him.

He had made such things. He had made delight.

HE SEES IT NOW, HE'S SURE, THROUGH GREEN, SOMETHING HE CAN plunge through. Soon he will be back there.

SIR?

WHITE SCALLOPS SPRING INTO THE SKY.

17

SATURDAY

Pruny arrives while Eileen's still asleep.

Auntie, Auntie, wake up, she whispers. Here's tea. And the paper. There. But be careful. Take a sip. There's news.

She lights Eileen a cigarette and sits down quietly across the room.

In her nightdress, under her ceiling eye, Eileen holds newsprint in shaking fingers and reads.

Like a stone dropping inside her.

A photo of a dog on a roof. And a picture of him, Le Grand, striding into the water, taken only a few days ago.

Eileen and Pruny look at each other across the room. Quiet. Burning tobacco.

Two men describe how they saw him struggling in the cove. Called from the rocks, couldn't reach him, waited until the waves pushed him close, hauled him in.

But that's not his dog, Eileen suddenly says. His dog died years ago.

Something heavy in her ribs.

Auntie. Are you all right?

A wave of her hand and she steps out to the terrace. Fingers on the railing, she stares southwest.

He'd left the cabanon and walked along the path, down the steps, over the pebbles, and swum. An hour later, been pulled from the water, carried over the rocks, away.

Soon he'll really be gone. They'll take him from Cap M to Paris. A procession, hoopla. He said he detested that sort of thing. Parades, processions, displays of his coffin at his monastery and chapel and other places he'd made as they drive him slowly to Paris. There they'll burn him. Then bring him back, carry him up the hill, plant him next to Von.

Up there he'll be like his Magdalene in that cave chapel he'd wanted to make, that earthen basilica looking out to sea. Drill a tunnel through a mountain, and there let Magdalene haunt until angels carry her upward.

Another creature left haunting.

She grips the rail. Because here she still is. In the sun, the heat, looking at vines, and lemon trees, and ancient Alps, and sea. She was the first, and here she still is.

INSIDE, SHE READS THE ARTICLE AGAIN. TAKES HER BLADE AND shakily cuts the piece free, smooths the crease with a ruler. Opens her cahier, pastes it in. No caption. It will not be the final item.

THEY'LL DRIVE HIM AWAY ON MONDAY. SHE WON'T WATCH THE PROcession. But will know as you feel these things, feel currents around you, when it passes.

Everyone will be gone, she thinks. The woman who now owns the villa will go to Paris for the funeral, and the old fish man and his wife and son. The dog: perhaps he will stay.

I don't think you need me to go with you now, says Pruny.

18

MONDAY

Since dawn Eileen's been thinly asleep. Sheets tangled with legs, she leans on an elbow, cranks open the ceiling eye. Scratch, flame, slow spiral of smoke.

Out of bed, to the washroom, turn faucets to a rush of water, let nightdress drop to ankles, step into the white-tiled tub. Clear green water rings her body in zones: breasts, knees. Head resting on the tiled ledge, eyes shut, she sees his bathtub at Villa S, blue tile and white, angles meeting the body. So beautiful. Slim elegant white house floating on thin legs in a meadow, then up the white ramp to the rooftop to look through a white frame of valley. So beautiful! Enough to make you cry, and she had, when she went, when she drove there. He was building it just as she built her house by the sea.

She can say it to herself now: the two white houses, his in a meadow and hers on the sea, on the same page: linked.

OUT OF THE TUB NOW, DRESS WITH CARE. PRESSED TROUSERS, blouse, brooch.

A glimpse of reflection: austere, silver-haired woman, black glass over one eye. A surprise to see self each time, when I am not old inside, she thinks, inside still a girl crouching to study snails in Brownswood, or wondering when Father'd come home again, or stroking Domino's fur in the sun, or trying so hard to see into Damia's brown eyes, into Bado's.

What do you think, she asks.

Pruny regards her and nods.

Bag, keys. Now out to the terrace, along the white gangway, down narrow steps to the car.

Look up to the terrace toward Pruny, dark halo of hair, her wave a salute.

Down the steep twisting road. Through town, roads cramped with cars and trucks and exhaust, then out again to the arc of beach and up along the narrow leafy road of the cape, past the ancient olive grove, down to park at the train station.

Pause a moment, quiet. Then climb out, cross the tracks with their tang of tar and dung, follow the path running between the train tracks and the earthen terraces that drop to the rocks, the sea.

What if she'd chosen another place that day?

Or if no Bado?

Along the tracks, beneath eucalypts and pines and morning glories, oh the wonderful morning air. Then past the steps down to the cove, and past the next steps, too, the ones that lead to her house. No, she'll walk by it for the moment. She'll go first to his.

NOW SHE'S THERE, AT THE SWEEP OF SHALLOW CONCRETE STEPS he made down to his earthen terrace. The cicadas are winding like clocks, and you can never see one, never, she's tried, peering into branches toward the noise. But always it's just the sound winding louder to a pitch, then falling, sound flowing from needles and bark.

Down the steps now. Down you go. They are appealing, she has to admire them, not like the steep narrow ones between sets of terracing but shallow and sweeping in a curve as if they'd take you to a ballroom. Yet to something so simple, an earthen terrace with a pair of cabins.

Here is his workshop, its corrugated roof strewn with yucca petals. Around it more yuccas, dracaenas, aloes, cactuses, squashed red cactus fruits. Then the ground drops in tangled green to the razory rocks, waves rolling in. Green-blue sea, the waves in shining arcs rolling from the deep, carving this cove, the next.

Behind her a train rattles by rattles

She waits until it's gone, quiet again. Just the cicadas, breeze, wash of pebbles below.

Here's the door of the workshop.

The door gives. Inside, darkness, smell of old man, pencil, and wood. Also something sharp. Push the door farther with a toe, step in. Morning light falls through the doorway. Now that can see a bit more, reach over table to unlatch a shutter to a tumble of light. A worktable here, smaller one by the door. On it a pair of bones. And a pinecone, shell, and rock.

A large old man sitting here on a crate, looking out to Mediterranean, hand resting on one of these bones.

You old Magdalene, she thinks. Pondering the future? Or past?

And here's a book covered in fur. She runs her fingers through it. His dog. Kept close.

Out the window, below: she can just see her bedroom window, and above, the glass spiral.

Her initials shyly winding around Bado's forty years ago.

ALL RIGHT NOW. AWAY FROM THE WINDOW. PINNED TO THE WALL are sheets of trace paper, moving in the air. Drawings of women, their buttocks and bosoms. On the first sheet, and the one beneath (lift with fingertip), and the one beneath it, too: nearly the same drawing, lines shifting a little. Solving a problem. Obsessed with a problem. An assembly of three figures: like the one on her wall?

Perhaps he was trying to please you, Bado said. Think of that?

She steps back toward the door and knocks into something. A clank and slosh, zig of wet on her ankle.

Out in the brightness she leans down to wipe it. White wet on her fingertip.

Paint.

NOW OVER THE NARROW PATH TO THE CABIN. ROUGH LOGS, SMALL square mirrored shutter, palm frond fixed to the door. Gently nudge it open.

I was invited.

And will never know why.

there's something I'd like no I need now to show you

Inside, the only light comes through the doorway behind her; she's a shadow peering into a slot. At its end, colored pegs are poked into the wood. Trousers hang on one, a rope. Pass through the narrow slot. Beside her the wall is painted, blue yellow, a figure, a fish or a bull or something, coiling black hairs, bristles and horns, so sudden and close—

She steps quickly back outside, shuts the door.

Enough of this place.

Back toward the workshop, in the doorway the can of white paint.

No, it's not paint.

It's primer.

something I'd like no I need now to show you

FEELING CURIOUSLY LIGHT NOW, CURIOUSLY LIGHT, SHE TURNS AND drifts up the ballroom stairs, along the path beneath shady trees, past the fish place, beyond.

To the narrow concrete steps that lead down to her house.

They've gone mossy in the corners, shadowed in long tongues of leaf. She steps down to the gate, pushes it, steps in.

Strange how places that have been sublimated into memory nevertheless still exist in the world.

The place jostles as she walks forward. The place and a slurry of moments.

She's just before the entrance now. One step up, turn to the right, and she is at her door.

And there it is. Yellow and red bosoms, large clasped hands, womanly hips aslant, tiny slitted triangle. A small face, blank staring eye.

Beneath her own *Enter slowly.*

She looks for a time, arms crossed, just looks.

Well, she thinks, you are hideous.

But

You've been in my life a long time.

She studies the painting, the inscrutable stripes and circles, and one quiet passage, a plane of moss green.

Then reaches up, holds her hand before the painting. And carefully places her palm over the woman's staring eye.

Rancor still rattles inside.

But like everything, so old.

She presses her palm to the painting, pauses, then blows carefully upon the back of her hand, between and around her fingers.

There.

Below, water rushes through, washes through, pebbles.

The weather's changing; Eileen looks up. The sky's gone pale. Through the lace of eucalypts and pines there's a sea haze of salt air and light, whiting away the sun.

ACKNOWLEDGMENTS

My thanks first to Alex Wall, who told me this story over a decade ago, launching me on a voyage of research and imagining. In addition to the buildings, objects, paintings, drawings, and written texts of Le Corbusier, Eileen Gray, and Jean Badovici, I've drawn from the work of many architectural scholars and biographers to develop this book (and, like most novelists, chosen on occasion to stretch or slide through facts). Among the authors to whom I'm most indebted are Peter Adam, Jean-Louis Cohen, Beatriz Colomina, Caroline Constant, Jennifer Goff, Sylvia Lavin, and Nicholas Fox Weber. The works of others were also invaluable, among them Tim Benton, Bruno Chiambretto, William J. R. Curtis, Rosamund Diamond, Deborah Gans, Philippe Garner, Stefan Hecker and Christian Müller, Richard Ingersoll, L. Stewart Johnson, Jean Paul Rayon, Flora Samuel, and Stanislaus van Moos.

Great, great gratitude to my agent, Emily Forland, and my editor, Gina Iaquinta, along with Peter Miller, Nick Curley, Maria Connors, Clio Hamilton, Sarahmay Wilkinson, and the rest of the team at Liveright/Norton; Helen Chandler for her incisive read; Manolita Farolan for the gracious loan of her Paris flat; the University of Miami for supporting early research; the University of Virginia for a sabbatical and two summers of later research; and the Joseph and Robert Cornell Foundation for a generous fellowship that let me write.

Finally, for all his insight and support, from the last swim in the cove to the last written word, my love and thanks to Edward Tuck.